$\mathcal{K}$eith asked me to be his assistant," Daphne revealed, not meeting Taylor's eyes.

"That's great!" Taylor cried. "Congratulations! Will he pay a lot?"

"The pay is excellent, plus Mandy will get free board."

Taylor blinked, not quite understanding. "Board? You already board her at Wildwood."

"But this would be free, and it's so much nicer."

"Are you saying you would leave Wildwood Stables?"

"It's a great opportunity," Daphne replied, and Taylor thought she heard a defensive note in her friend's voice.

"You would still give lessons at Wildwood, wouldn't you?" Taylor asked, growing concerned.

"I might not be able to," Daphne said, looking away.

Ride over to
WILDWOOD STABLES

WILDWOOD STABLES
Taking the Leap

BY SUZANNE WEYN

SCHOLASTIC INC.
New York   Toronto   London   Auckland
Sydney   Mexico City   New Delhi   Hong Kong

No part of this publication may be reproduced, stored in a retrieval system, or transmitted in any form or by any means, electronic, mechanical, photocopying, recording, or otherwise, without written permission of the publisher. For information regarding permission, write to: Scholastic Inc., Attention: Permissions Department, 557 Broadway, New York, NY 10012.

ISBN 978-0-545-23092-6

12 11 10 9 8 7 6 5 4 3 2 1   11 12 13 14 15 16/0

Printed in the U.S.A.   40
First printing, February 2011

With love to **Becca Weyn**, the family's next horse girl.

And with special thanks to **Diana Gonzalez**, who has contributed to this series in so many ways. This is her story and without her help, I couldn't have written these books.

WILDWOOD STABLES

Taking the Leap

Chapter 1

"Pay attention to your diagonals," Keith Hobbes reminded thirteen-year-old Taylor Henry as she trotted around the indoor ring at Ross River Ranch. The renowned riding instructor stood in the center of the ring with his arms folded, watching. He was dressed as always in a black T-shirt, tan breeches, and polished tall black boots. He pushed back his brimmed cap, revealing tufts of white hair.

Taylor struggled to recall what Keith had taught her about diagonals. Although she was a confident Western rider, she was new to English riding. What was it he'd taught her during their last session? Slowing to a walk, Taylor tried to remember.

When she was traveling clockwise in a ring, as she was at that moment, she should be rising out of her stirrups while the horse's front outside leg swung forward.

Was she on the correct diagonal now? Taylor wasn't sure.

Taylor picked up a sitting trot once again. She checked the shoulder of the mare she was riding. Serafina, a black quarter horse with a white blaze, belonged to Ross River Ranch. The horse's leg was back when she rose out of the saddle, which wasn't what Taylor — or Keith Hobbes — wanted.

To get onto the correct diagonal, Taylor would have to change position. But how?

Then she remembered what Keith had told her to do. To get her posting into the correct sit-rise-sit rhythm, she sat for an extra beat and then rose into the post as soon as Serafina's shoulder went back.

"That's it!" Keith encouraged her. "Good girl!"

Taylor beamed at her instructor, proud of earning his approval. She had so much respect for Keith, who was a retired United States Equestrian Federation judge, an A circuit competitor, and a former Olympic dressage team trainer. Winning these free lessons was one of the best things that had ever happened to her. On her own, she could never have afforded to train with him.

A lithe, willowy girl with long, silky black hair entered the spectator area outside the ring. Taylor recognized her immediately. Smiling, she waved.

Daphne Chang was the sixteen-year-old riding instructor over at Wildwood Stables. She boarded her gray speckled mare, Mandy, across the aisle from Taylor's black quarter horse gelding, Prince Albert, and Pixie, the palomino Shetland pony mare. Taylor had acquired Prince Albert and Pixie in a rescue and now worked for their board at the newly opened rustic ranch.

Daphne returned Taylor's wave but didn't smile as Taylor would have expected her to. Taylor's brow furrowed in worried confusion. What was wrong with Daphne?

"Okay, Taylor, that's enough for today. You can walk out and relax," Keith called as he approached Daphne with a friendly smile. "Nice job."

"Thanks!" Taylor hadn't realized Daphne knew Keith,

but remembered that Daphne had boarded Mandy at Ross River before she brought the Arabian-barb mix over to Wildwood. That was probably how she knew the trainer.

Taylor slowed Serafina to a walk to let her cool down before bringing her back to be groomed by the ranch's stable hands. Ross River Ranch was so different from Wildwood Stables, where all the riders did their own grooming and tacking. Everything was luxurious at Ross River.

Trying not to be too obvious, Taylor cut her eyes over to where Daphne sat with Keith. They were in a deep discussion. Then they both stood and shook hands.

Keith left, exiting to the outside. Daphne stood and waited as Taylor approached, still riding Serafina at a walk.

"What was that about?" Taylor asked.

"Keith asked me to be his assistant," Daphne revealed, not meeting Taylor's eyes.

"That's great!" Taylor cried. "That's wonderful. Congratulations! There's no one better than Keith. You'll learn so much. Not that you need to."

"Are you kidding?" Daphne replied. "I'll learn so much about training and instructing. To work with Keith Hobbes is the chance of a lifetime."

"Will he pay a lot?" Taylor asked.

"The pay is excellent, plus Mandy will get free board."

Taylor blinked, not quite understanding. "Board? You already board her at Wildwood."

"But this would be free, and it's so much nicer here."

"Are you saying you would leave Wildwood Stables?"

"It's a great opportunity," Daphne replied, and Taylor thought she heard a defensive note in her friend's voice.

"You would still give lessons at Wildwood, wouldn't you?" Taylor asked, growing concerned.

"I might not be able to," Daphne said, looking away.

A knot of anxiety began to grow in Taylor's stomach. "What are we going to do? We won't have any instructors!" she exclaimed.

Daphne looked back at Taylor, guilt in her eyes. "I'll try to help you guys find a new one, but" — she paused and took a deep breath, and with a self-assuring nod finished — "but I am definitely taking this position."

Taylor nodded back, tight-lipped. Before Taylor could think of something to say, Daphne looked away and mumbled, "I'm sorry. I'll see you later." She strode off toward the office, leaving Taylor still on Serafina, in the ring.

Taking a steadying breath, Taylor dismounted and led Serafina to the barn. Her mind raced with possible solutions. Was it in Wildwood's budget to hire another trainer? Without an instructor, would they lose a lot of business from lessons?

Around the corner of the barn, in the round pen, was a man in a wheelchair speaking to another man. The standing man, who wore jeans and a blue shirt, held on to a lead rope, while an anxious-looking bay pranced back and forth on the other end.

Taylor's eyebrows shot up in surprise when the horse reared and began to dart in circles around the circular pen. The man in the blue shirt started forward after the bay, only to be stopped by a halting gesture from the man in the wheelchair. Taylor recognized the wheelchair-bound man as Jim LeFleur, the son of Mrs. LeFleur, owner of Wildwood Stables.

Taylor knew that Jim LeFleur had been an avid rider before a terrible jumping accident that had left him paralyzed from the waist down. Taylor wondered what he was doing in there, and if it was even safe for him to be that close to a rearing horse. Filled with a burning curiosity, she crept closer, still holding on to Serafina.

"Just let him go, Rob. Let him make a few laps and get out some energy before trying anything else," Jim LeFleur advised the man who was standing. Rob, who Taylor gathered was the standing man, nodded and watched as the horse ran circles around the metal pole walls of the pen.

"Good. *Now* you can put the lunge line on him. Slowly now, don't make any sudden movements," Jim continued to instruct, "and don't look him in the eyes. Remember, he's a prey animal, and eye contact is a predatory move to him. We want to seem friendly and nonthreatening, not like we're going to eat him."

Rob nodded once again and approached the horse, moving very slowly. When he reached the now slightly sweaty bay, he stroked his neck with the lunge line, showing the horse he meant no harm. Reaching forward, he clipped the line under the horse's chin. Rob paused and looked to Jim for further instruction. Jim nodded to him and said, "Nice. Now get him working on the rail."

Taylor had been so engrossed with watching the men train the horse that she jumped when she felt a hot puff of breath on her neck. Whipping around, she saw Serafina, who had been nibbling on the back of her jacket. Serafina jumped back a bit, as startled by Taylor's sudden movement as Taylor had been by the horse's.

Taylor chuckled and petted Serafina's soft nose. "Let's get you back to the barn so you can rest, hmm?" she said. As Taylor continued her walk back to the barn she wondered about Jim's situation with his mother and Devon Ross. Taylor knew that he no longer interacted with Mrs. LeFleur, and he called Devon Ross "Aunt Devon." Taylor was also aware that Devon Ross and Mrs. LeFleur were cousins who were not on good terms. Why did Jim work for the often icy Devon Ross instead of his own mother, who was so welcoming? What had happened in their past to make those relationships so strained?

Glancing over her shoulder to the round pen, Taylor marveled at how confident Jim still was with horses. Despite being in a wheelchair, he clearly knew what he was doing and worked with the confidence of an experienced rider. He'd obviously had enough belief in his ability to continue his work with horses after the accident. He seemed to truly have a gift and a passion for horses. If only Taylor could find someone who had an equally strong gift and passion for teaching riding lessons to replace Daphne!

Walking into the high-ceilinged, spacious, clean Ross River stables, Taylor greeted a neatly dressed man in polished paddock boots and a white polo shirt embroidered with the ranch's logo. He looked to be in his forties, but he was only a little taller than Taylor. "Hi, Enrique. How are you today?"

"Very well, thank you. Did you have a good lesson?" Enrique asked. He had a slight Spanish accent and a friendly, weathered face.

Taylor nodded. "Keith is so great," she replied.

Enrique extended a rough, leathery hand to take

Serafina's reins from Taylor. As always, Taylor noticed that he smelled of soap and hay. He smiled at her once more, clipped Serafina to the cross ties, and walked into a room down the aisle, on the left.

Enrique was such a nice, gentlemanly man, and so kind to the horses. Taylor realized that she would miss him once her lessons here ended, which would be soon. She only had one left. Ross River Ranch really was a nice place, even though Taylor's heart would always belong to Wildwood Stables. In a way she could see why Daphne would want to board Mandy here.

Taylor cut her thought short. No. Daphne was part of Wildwood. That's where she and Mandy belonged. After Daphne thought about it some more, she would realize she just couldn't leave Wildwood. And if she didn't realize it on her own, Taylor would have to find a way to convince her.

In one of the stalls, Taylor noticed a light gray, nearly white horse she'd never seen there before. She was sure of it because she would certainly have remembered a horse like this one. It was huge — easily seventeen hands high — with massively broad withers and a thick neck!

And yet for such a big horse, its legs were surprisingly short.

Enrique came by, holding his grooming box so he could brush down Serafina. He stopped and smiled at Taylor's awestruck expression. "That's a French horse," he told her. "A Percheron. Would you believe the big fellow has Arabian blood in him?"

Taylor stepped closer to the horse. "I can't see it," she admitted.

"When he walks you can see it in his gait. He walks like an Arabian," Enrique told her.

Taylor thought of Shafir, the playful young Arabian mare that lived at Wildwood Stables. She pictured the fine-boned chestnut horse's free-flowing, delicate stride. There was no way Taylor could picture this massive animal moving with such grace.

"He moves so well. That's what makes him good at pulling heavy things," Enrique added.

"He's a draft horse?" Taylor asked.

"Of course he's a draft," Enrique cried with a good-natured laugh. "Look at the size of him! He's a giant. Mrs. Ross just bought him."

Taylor read the engraved nameplate outside the Percheron's stall: JACQUES. Taylor laughed. "Of course he'd be named Jacques. He's French!"

"Vive la France!" Enrique joked.

"Why does Mrs. Ross need a draft horse?" Taylor asked. Whenever she'd seen Mrs. Ross riding, she was on a gorgeous Thoroughbred. "What does she need to pull?"

"She doesn't have to pull anything, but why not?" Enrique countered. "He's a beauty. Mrs. Ross loves beautiful horses, and she has the fortune to buy what she loves."

Enrique moved on down the aisle toward Serafina. His words still played in Taylor's head: *Mrs. Ross has the fortune to buy what she loves.*

Had Devon Ross bought her nephew's love — somehow taken his affection from Mrs. LeFleur? Was that why Mrs. LeFleur could never forgive her cousin?

Chapter 2

"Hey, Mrs. LeFleur, what's up?" Taylor asked as she hit the answer button on her phone. She looked up from her math homework, happy to have a distraction.

"Hi, Taylor," Mrs. LeFleur said. "Could you do me a big favor and give the horses their evening feeding tonight? I can't get through to Mercedes. I'm not sure if she's already there, or if she just has bad cell phone reception at home, too."

Either was possible. Whenever Taylor was in the back pasture at Wildwood, her cell phone showed almost no bars. Taylor didn't usually have a problem getting ahold of Mercedes, another junior manager at Wildwood Stables, at home, but sometimes phone reception was tricky in Pheasant Valley.

Taylor glanced back down at her unfinished math homework. She could always do it when she got back; it was only four o'clock now.

"I'll ask my mom if I can get a ride down there and then call you right back, okay?"

"Sure thing, thanks," Mrs. LeFleur said, hanging up.

Taylor snapped her math textbook shut and walked downstairs to where her mother was working in the kitchen. Taylor's mom had begun her own catering business, which she worked on when she wasn't on duty as a waitress at the Pheasant Valley Diner. In her free time, she was always trying new recipes to entice possible clients.

"Mmm . . . smells good in here!" Taylor said as she came up behind her mother, who was looking down into the large, simmering, cast-iron pot of red Manhattan-style clam chowder on the stove.

Her mother jumped at Taylor's sudden appearance. "You scared me!" Jennifer Henry chuckled and wiped her brow, looking at her daughter. She tucked a blonde curl back into her headband.

"Would you mind driving me down to Wildwood?" Taylor asked her. "Mrs. LeFleur needs someone to do evening feeding."

Jennifer sighed thoughtfully. "I'm working a five o'clock shift at the diner tonight. I can drop you off on the way into work, I guess."

"Oh, and can Travis come over at seven?" Taylor added quickly. "We were planning to play Zombie Quest tonight. Mrs. LeFleur will give me a ride home." Travis Ryan was Taylor's best friend in the world.

"Is your homework done?" her mother asked, looking back to the steaming vat of soup and giving it another stir.

Taylor hesitated before admitting, "Well . . . mostly. But I can finish it later tonight."

"How late?"

"After Zombie Quest?" Taylor asked hopefully.

Her mother stopped stirring and looked pointedly at Taylor. "If working at the barn and playing video games are going to start affecting your grades, we're going to need to come up with a schedule or something. Times when you can go to the barn and times when you have to be focusing on schoolwork."

"But, Mom! It's just this one time. Mrs. LeFleur called me and asked me to do her a favor. And don't worry, I've been doing well in all my classes," Taylor insisted. *Except for math,* she added silently in her head, giving her mother the best puppy eyes she could manage.

"Maybe you should cancel with Travis," Jennifer suggested.

"He'll only stay an hour," Taylor negotiated. "And isn't Claire coming tonight to use your printer? She'll be here, too."

Her mother clapped her hand over her forehead. "I forgot Claire was coming. But that will work out." She sighed and glanced down at her soup. "Fine," she conceded. "But I want to look over your homework when you're done."

"Deal!" Taylor shouted, and dashed down the hall to get her boots on.

Taylor and her mother rumbled down the gravel driveway to Wildwood Stables, a plume of dirt following behind them. The sun cast slanted shadows across the ground before them, and Taylor noted how it seemed to be getting dark so much earlier these days. Although there had been no snow yet, the gray clouds above them threatened to let lose their white flurries any day now.

When her mother stopped the car, Taylor hurried out, giving Jennifer a quick peck on the cheek. Walking toward the barn, she could see to her right that Mercedes *was* there, working an all-white Missouri Fox Trotting horse on a lunge line. The horse trotted in circles as Mercedes stood in the center, lunge line in one hand, lunge whip in the other.

Taylor walked up to the rail, putting one leg up on the wood and watching. Montana Wind Dancer was the gelding's registered name, but everyone called him by his barn name, Monty.

Monty had once belonged to Mercedes. She'd trained

him herself, back when her family lived in Connecticut and owned a whole stable of horses. But when the Gonzalez family fell on hard times, their stable was sold, and Monty, along with the other horses, went to a new home. He was resold a few months earlier, this time to Ross River Ranch. Mercedes discovered him again when Taylor started taking lessons at Ross River. When Mrs. Ross saw how wonderful Mercedes was with Monty, she asked the girl to work with him more over here at Wildwood.

It was too good to be true, and Taylor sometimes wondered if it *was* true. Had Devon Ross taken pity on Mercedes? Had she noticed how much Mercedes loved and missed Monty? Mrs. Ross didn't come across as the softhearted type, but still . . .

Mercedes smiled and jerked her chin in greeting as she rotated in circles with the horse. Taylor waved and ducked under the rail, entering the ring.

"So you *are* here!" Taylor said, grinning, happy to see that Mercedes was happy as well. Mercedes tugged gently on the lunge line, bringing Monty to a stop, and gave Taylor a quizzical look.

"Of course I'm here," she said, unclipping the lunge line from over Monty's nose and reclipping it under his chin to lead him. "Where else would I be?"

"Mrs. LeFleur called and asked me to do evening feeding because she wasn't sure if you were here or not."

Mercedes's hand went into one of her front jean pockets, then the other. Her brow furrowed and then released in realization. "Oh! My phone must be in the office. I was so excited to get to see Monty that I must have left it there. Sorry you had to come all the way down here." She patted Monty's slightly damp neck. His nostrils still flaring from the workout, Monty made a soft spluttering noise, as if to say, *Phew! What a day!*

Taylor grinned at the charismatic horse. Whatever had inspired her to do so, it was really nice of Devon Ross to let Mercedes bring Monty over to Wildwood to work with him.

Looking back at Mercedes, Taylor said, "I don't mind. It's always nice to have an excuse to come see the horses. I'll help you feed later. Always helps to have more hands."

Just then, another car came down the driveway. Taylor's stomach gave a little jump of excitement when she recognized Eric Mason heading their way. The small flame of enthusiasm was quickly extinguished when she noticed who was sitting next to him — his cousin Plum.

Taylor waved at them both. She was determined to be nice to Plum, even if it killed her. By not giving Plum any ammo, Taylor hoped she was protecting herself from the girl's sneering meanness. It was also awkward with Eric — whom she liked so much — when she and Plum were at war. It would be easier for everyone to get along if she and Plum could at least be civil with each other.

And there was a third reason not to fight with Plum. This was Wildwood Stables, after all. People should help one another and be friendly in the best place in the world. Taylor wondered if she was being silly for feeling that the ranch should be better, friendlier, warmer than other places, but it was how she felt, just the same.

Eric smiled and waved back, walking over toward Taylor. Each time Taylor saw him she was impressed all over again with his bright eyes, dark hair, and broad shoulders. And he was nice, too. She was always happy to see him.

Plum gave a curt smile, her eyes still glaring. Tossing back her blonde hair, she adjusted one of the diamond stud earrings she always wore and quickly headed to Shafir's stall without saying a word to any of them. Taylor was too distracted by Eric's smile to give Plum any notice.

"Hey, kiddo, how're you doing?" Eric said.

Kiddo. *Kiddo?! Kiddo* was *not* the term of endearment she was hoping for. He *was* three years older than her, after all . . . but *kiddo?*

"Uh, doing well. Just came down here to help feed," Taylor said, and glanced at the paddock where Spots and a new horse, Forest, were grazing. Spots was the fawn they'd rescued after Taylor spied his mother lying dead on the side of the road. He'd been at the barn for nearly two months. At first they'd made him a home inside the tack room; the week before, he'd gotten big enough that they had moved him to a stall. Eric used to come just to feed him goat's milk from a bottle. Later they added bananas to the goat's milk. Now the baby deer was drinking from a feeder they'd set up in the paddock.

"Spots is getting really big, huh?" Taylor observed.

"I'm happy that he and Forest get along, but we need to find another place for him to live."

"I'm really surprised Spots hasn't decided to run away," Eric said. "Maybe he doesn't know he is a deer."

Taylor chuckled. "Yeah, maybe he thinks he's just a very tiny pony."

Out of the corner of her eye, Taylor saw Plum walk out of the barn with Shafir, the gorgeous young chestnut-colored Arabian mare she leased from the ranch. Plum stood with her arms crossed, tapping her foot with impatience.

"Come *on*!" Plum shouted to Eric.

Eric turned, made a shooing motion with his hands, and called back, "Go and warm up! I'll be right there!" He then turned back to Taylor. "We're going to go on a trail ride. Would you and Prince Albert like to join?"

"Think Plum would mind?" asked Taylor, not really caring if Plum *did* mind. She was so excited that Eric had asked her to join them that Plum's poutiness wouldn't be a problem. Eric glanced over at Plum, who had mounted Shafir and was walking around the ring.

"Uh, I don't think so," he said. Eric tried to stay out of the middle when it came to Plum and Taylor, even though he certainly knew they didn't like each other.

Plum rounded the corner so she could see them and mouthed, "Hurry up!" to Eric.

Eric held up a finger in a "just a minute" gesture and looked back at Taylor again. "So?" he prompted.

Taylor grinned. "I'll go get Prince Albert ready. I can't go far, though. I promised to help Mercedes with the last feeding."

Eric smiled back. "We'll just go out for a short while. It will be dark before long, anyway," he said.

"Okay," Taylor agreed.

Taylor turned toward the stalls and headed in the direction of Prince Albert, when Mercedes popped her head out of the office door.

"Hey, Taylor!" she called, smiling and shaking her cell phone back and forth.

Taylor turned her head and looked at Mercedes. "What's up?" she called back.

"I'm on a mass text list for Ross River Ranch updates,

and I just got a message saying that they're having another competition! The beginners are already filled up, but there's still room in the upper division classes."

"I'm still pretty much a beginner," Taylor said. She was excited to hear about another competition so soon after her first real riding event, at which she'd done well. She wasn't sure she was ready to move out of the beginner division, though.

"You won that class you competed in as if you had been riding English for years," Mercedes pointed out. "We should both enter this one! And guess what the prize is?"

Taylor shrugged and guessed, "A ribbon?"

"Nope! Even more lessons with Keith Hobbes!"

Taylor's eyebrows shot up. More lessons with Keith? He was a great instructor, and she had really begun to improve with just the few lessons she'd already had. There was no way she could afford to keep taking lessons with him, however. But if she won this competition, it would give her a chance to keep training with him.

Could she handle a higher level? The competition would be stiffer, and the jumps would be a lot higher and even more dangerous. Still, the prize would be well worth the effort. She just didn't know if she could do it. Oh, but to keep studying with Keith — she wanted to keep on so badly it made her stomach clench with longing.

Was she brave enough to give it a shot?

Chapter 3

O h, man!" Taylor shouted, smacking her plastic controller down on her living room couch in frustration. "How do you always make it past those zombies?"

Travis Ryan, a heavyset boy with short-cropped white blond hair, grinned, though he kept his blue eyes fixed intently on the video game playing in front of them. "After a while I just know when they're going to pop out," he said. "I can almost feel it."

Taylor's muscles ached from the ranch chores combined with the trail ride. Plum had been icy when she saw Taylor emerge from the stable mounted on Prince Albert, all set to join Plum and Eric on their ride. But Taylor had just smiled and hung back behind Jojo, Eric's Tennessee walking horse. She'd gotten back from the trail just in time to help Mercedes. It was dark before Mrs. LeFleur locked up and drove Taylor home.

A wild-eyed zombie appeared on the screen, and Travis's avatar hurled a fireball in his direction. The zombie instantly vanished. "All right!" Travis shouted. As his video character disappeared through a door, he turned toward Taylor. "See you at the next level," he said with a laugh.

"If I ever get there," Taylor moaned.

Travis reached out for Taylor's controller. "Want me to bring you up a level?" he offered.

"Okay," Taylor agreed as she put the plastic controller in his hand.

Taylor watched as her best friend expertly sped her video avatar through the obstacle course of attacking zombies. She and Travis hadn't spent time together like this in a while. Sometimes Travis helped out at the barn. He was good at repairing things. Lately, though, he hadn't been coming down to Wildwood as often, so it felt good to just hang out with him at her house like they'd done before Prince Albert, Pixie, and Wildwood Stables had become such a huge part of Taylor's life.

Taylor's avatar disappeared behind the door, and the screen flashed: LEVEL TWO COMPLETE!!! "Thanks," she said to Travis. "I'd never have gotten out of there without you. I'm no good at this game."

"You're usually good at it," he disagreed. "Not as good as me, but better than you just were. Your mind wasn't on it. What's up?"

He knew her so well. That was no surprise. They'd been friends since elementary school.

"It's this hunter-jumper event that's coming up at Ross River Ranch," Taylor told him. "If I can win it, I'll get to extend my lessons with Keith. He's such an awesome teacher, and I'm learning so much from him."

"So what's the problem?" Travis asked. "You've been doing well in these events so far."

"The beginner level is full, so I'd have to compete in a higher division than before."

Travis let out a hoot of laughter. "Just like in the video game."

Taylor smiled and nodded. "I guess it is sort of like that," she allowed. "I just don't know if I'm ready for that level."

"Oh, you're ready," Travis said confidently. "You're just nervous. You can totally do it. And think about this — Plum has been competing at the beginner level, so you won't have to deal with her."

"That's true," Taylor agreed. Plum was definitely capable of entering competitions at a higher level, but Taylor was fairly sure that the girl stayed in the beginner category just so she could beat Taylor. So far it hadn't worked.

"There's another thing," Taylor added. "All these events have entry fees. I hate always asking Mom for the money."

"Try your dad," Travis suggested. Taylor's parents were divorced.

Taylor shook her head. "He's always complaining that Mike, his boss at the repair garage, isn't giving him enough work, and so he doesn't have enough money. I asked him if he could pay for winter blankets for Pixie and Prince Albert and he said he just couldn't do it."

"Don't they have blankets already?" Travis asked.

Taylor shook her head sadly. "Those blankets Eric got turned out to be stolen property, remember?"

"Oh, yeah. I forgot," Travis said.

"We gave all the stolen horse stuff back," Taylor continued.

"What a dope," Travis said.

Taylor knew he was talking about Eric. Travis made no secret that he didn't like Eric, even though Eric had never done anything to Travis. Taylor and Travis had been best friends for so long that Taylor suspected that Travis was jealous of her growing friendship with Eric. "He's not a dope," Taylor defended Eric.

"Yeah, whatever," Travis grumbled.

The front door opened, and Taylor's mother walked in. She was still dressed in the black pants and white shirt she wore for her waitress job at the Pheasant Valley Diner.

"You're home kind of early," Taylor noted. She glanced at the clock on the cable box below their TV. "Two whole hours early." Then she noticed that her mother looked pale and tired. "Are you sick?" Taylor asked, suddenly worried.

Jennifer threw herself down heavily into a stuffed armchair across from Taylor and Travis. "I got laid off," she revealed in a tired, defeated tone.

"They fired you?" Taylor gasped. "What did you do?"

Her mother smiled wearily. "I didn't *do* anything! Being laid off is different from being fired. Business has been slow lately, so they had to let someone go. Everyone has worked there longer than I have, so — there's a saying, 'Last hired, first fired.'"

"But I thought you weren't fired," Travis pointed out.

"I know, but you get the idea," Jennifer said. "'First laid off' wouldn't rhyme. It's just an expression."

"Sorry," Taylor said in a small voice. "At least you'll have more time for the catering business, right?"

Jennifer had been working hard to get her catering business going, though they still counted on the money she made as a waitress to pay their bills.

"I'm not so sure we can count on that. I haven't booked a party in a while, and I have nothing coming up," Jennifer remarked. She stood and took her cell phone from her pocket. "Did you eat?" she asked Taylor.

"The clam chowder was awesome," Taylor reported.

Jennifer headed into the small den off the living room where her best friend, Claire Black, was using her printer. "Guess what they did to me at the diner," Taylor and Travis heard Jennifer say before the door closed behind her.

"Claire will cheer her up," Taylor said hopefully. "They've been friends since Pheasant Valley Elementary, just like we have." Claire Black was so close to the family that Taylor thought of her more as an aunt than as just her mom's friend.

"I wonder if we'll still be friends when we're old like them," Travis said.

Taylor didn't think her mother was considered old. She was somewhere in her thirties. But she understood what Travis meant.

Could she and Travis be friends that long? Would the boy-girl thing get in their way after a while?

Taylor hoped not, because she really loved Travis, but like a brother. The idea of them ever having any other kind of relationship was too strange to even imagine. She was pretty sure Travis felt the same way about her, though sometimes when Eric was around he'd act oddly jealous. Maybe Travis was just afraid that Eric wanted to take the best friend spot from him. "We'll always be friends," Taylor assured Travis.

"I think so, too," Travis agreed. "Want to see how you do at the third level? They have some kick-butt zombie ninjas on three."

"Sure," Taylor agreed.

Taylor tried to pay attention to the video game, but talking about friendship made her think about Daphne. Taylor had believed she and Daphne were friends, or at least fast on the way to becoming so. She'd also believed that Wildwood Stables meant as much to Daphne as it did to Taylor. But if that was the case, how could she move Mandy over to Ross River Ranch? Daphne knew how much Mrs. LeFleur needed every horse's boarding fee she could get. And who would teach lessons at Wildwood now?

How could Daphne betray them all like this?

"Now what's on your mind?" Travis asked in an exasperated tone. "That zombie ninja just vaporized you. You're not even paying attention."

A cloud of smoky video vapor shimmered in the spot where Taylor's avatar had stood only moments earlier. "Oops," Taylor said with a sheepish grin.

"Still worrying about the horse event?" Travis asked.

"Among other things," Taylor replied. She didn't feel like talking about what had happened with Daphne — not with Travis, anyway. He had a way of being very logical, and she wasn't in the mood for any arguments he might make. Taylor knew exactly how Travis thought. He'd say it was a great chance for Daphne, and Taylor couldn't expect her to turn it down.

Taylor didn't want to hear it. She wanted to be angry and to blame Daphne for being disloyal to Wildwood Stables.

"Like, what other things?" Travis asked.

"Well, Spots, for one thing," Taylor replied. This was true. Eric had worried her when he said he was surprised Spots hadn't run away. Did Spots *want* to run away? He *was* getting bigger. She hadn't noticed how very much larger he was until this afternoon.

The den door opened. "What about Spots?" Claire asked. A petite woman dressed in denim and with short brown hair, Claire smiled at them as she walked into the living room. She held a stack of flyers showing an adorable mother cat with her seven tiny kittens. Taylor knew that Claire would put these flyers all over Pheasant Valley until she'd found a home for each kitten.

Bunny, Claire's brindle-coated pit bull, followed Claire into the living room from the den and licked Taylor's hand. Travis reached over to scratch Bunny between her ears.

"Spots is getting sort of big," Taylor explained. "We've moved him from the tack room to a stall. But I don't think a deer belongs in a stall, do you?"

Claire rubbed the top of her head thoughtfully. "You're right. Spots must be at least ten to fourteen weeks old by now. We can't be exactly sure."

"Should we let him go?" Travis asked Claire.

Instead of answering him, Claire asked Taylor, "Does Spots still have his spots?"

"A few, but most of them have faded."

"Spots lost his mother before she could teach him to survive on his own in the wild," Claire explained. "It's too late for him to be able to survive on his own."

"So what do we do?" Taylor asked as Bunny came to sit by her feet.

"I've been in touch with a man who has a deer sanctuary upstate," Claire said.

"What's that?" Travis asked.

"He has acres of protected woods and fields. Deer can roam freely, but there aren't any predators. And they have an abundance of natural vegetation for the deer to eat," Claire answered.

"It's perfect for Spots!" Taylor cried happily.

"He only takes a limited number of deer," Claire cautioned. "He wants the deer he takes to be totally independent. Has Spots been sleeping outside?"

Taylor shook her head. "We give him some outside time in the day, but we put him in a stall at night."

"You might want to get him outside into one of the paddocks to sleep."

"But it's cold now," Taylor pointed out.

"Right," Claire said, "and he has to start building up a winter coat."

Jennifer came into the living room. "Did I hear you talking about that little deer at the ranch?" she asked.

"He's not so little anymore," Taylor told her mother.

Claire put her arm around Jennifer's shoulders. "Bad day at the diner is actually good news," she said.

Jennifer pulled out of her friend's embrace to gaze at her with a puzzled expression. "Maybe you didn't hear me correctly there in the den," she said. "I just lost my job."

"Exactly!" Claire cried with enthusiasm. "This is your golden opportunity. Now you can work on your catering full time and really get it off the ground. And what perfect timing! It's the holidays, and you know that means people are having luncheons and dinners and holiday parties."

"I've probably missed the season by now," Jennifer disagreed. "People have already booked their catering."

Claire pushed Jennifer lightly on the shoulder. "That's no attitude. You know there are always people who wait until the last minute."

"Mrs. LeFleur has been thinking about having a winter carnival down at the stables," Taylor said. Mrs. LeFleur had mentioned it just the day before. It would be a fundraiser to help the animals.

Jennifer's face brightened with interest. "Maybe I'll give her a call."

"Speaking of Mrs. LeFleur," Claire said, turning back to Taylor, "I rescued a feral cat who had a litter of kittens two months ago." Claire held up the flyers she'd just printed out in the den. "They're ready to be adopted out, and I don't want to keep them with my feral cats. Their mother is wild, but the kittens can be domesticated right away."

"Does living in a barn make them wild or domesticated?" Taylor asked.

"If people feed them and interact with them, they're considered domesticated," Claire replied. "Do you think Wildwood would keep them as barn cats?"

"Mice have been getting into the feed and sleeping in the hay," Taylor replied. "Mrs. LeFleur was saying she wanted to get some cats."

"Excellent. I'll go down there," Claire said.

"I'll go with you," Jennifer agreed. "I can see if Mrs. LeFleur wants catering help for her carnival."

Maybe her mother's business would boom and there would be money for entering the hunter-jumper event, Taylor thought hopefully. If things went well enough, Taylor might even find the nerve to ask her mother for money to buy winter blankets for Pixie and Prince Albert.

Chapter 4

Taylor puffed out a plume of hot breath into the cold air, watching it fade away in front of her. She didn't recall it being cold enough to see her breath the day before, but it *was* December. The holiday season was starting to get into swing. As she walked up to Prince Albert's stall, she wondered if he had ever received a Christmas gift.

"What do you want for Christmas, boy?" she asked, stroking the horse's black muzzle with a gloved hand. "Some treats? I know how much you like the apple-flavored ones."

Although it wasn't one of Taylor's assigned days to be at Wildwood, she had decided to take the bus after school with Travis, who was going over to help Eric fix a fence. She had made sure to finish her homework during her lunch period so that her mother would allow her to go. Well, at least she'd finished *most* of it.

Taylor had spent all day at school looking out the window at the bright azure of the sky, thinking how nice it would be to go on a trail ride. It would start snowing soon, and with no indoor ring at Wildwood, her riding time would be sharply reduced until next spring.

A sudden, loud banging noise made Prince Albert prick his ears and look in the direction the sound was coming from. Taylor followed his gaze to the top of the hill and saw Eric holding up a piece of fallen rail while Travis tried to hammer a nail into it. *Bang, bang, bang.* The noise echoed through the small valley, making the horses pick up their heads in response to the strange noise. *Bang, bang —*

"Ow!" Travis shouted, dropping the hammer and shaking his hand in pain. Taylor winced as she watched her friend proceed to shout and jump and give the rail a swift, angry kick. Eric winced as well, putting the rail down for a moment and descending the hill to lead Travis toward the office.

The noise made Mercedes, who was mucking stalls, come toward the front of the barn, plastic pitchfork in hand. Her eyes darted around as she asked, "Is everyone okay?"

Plum, who had been quietly cleaning her new jumping saddle on the mounting block, rolled her eyes. "Yeah, we're fine."

"Speak for yourself! I'm surprised my thumb isn't as flat as a pancake!" Travis shouted from the bottom of the hill, still shaking his hand in pain. Plum shrugged in response, going back to polishing her saddle.

Mercedes jerked a thumb toward the office and told Travis and Eric, "There's a medical kit in there if you need a cold pack or something."

Eric nodded. "Thanks. Come on, let's get you bandaged up."

"Stupid fence," Travis muttered.

Taylor walked over and took Travis's hand, examining

his thumb. It was red and painful looking but not too bad. Before she could comment on it, a sight behind Travis's shoulder caught her eye.

"Oh, my gosh!" Taylor shouted, pointing toward the paddock with Forest in it. "Spots, no!"

Everyone's heads snapped up, looking in the direction Taylor was pointing. Spots, tail held high like a white flag, was racing toward the fence. With a spectacular leap, the small deer cleared the fence and took off in the opposite direction of the hill.

Taylor felt as if she must be in a dream. The whole sight had been so unreal. But that dreamlike feeling quickly left her as the group, except for Plum, bolted after Spots.

"Come back!" Mercedes called, but then clapped her hand over her mouth. "Maybe we shouldn't shout. We might scare him more."

"Yeah, let's be quiet," Taylor agreed.

"We can catch him when he reaches the upper pasture," Eric suggested. "The fence gate is shut."

Eric, Taylor, Travis, and Mercedes ran toward the upper pasture, where Spots raced back and forth along the split-rail fence. His path was obstructed, and he was looking for a way in. "We'll catch up with him there," Eric said confidently.

Taylor hoped he was right. She didn't think the little deer would be so easy to catch. He was amazingly fast. And who knew he could jump like that? When had he developed *that* ability?

"Come on, Spots," Eric crooned as they got closer. "Calm down. We're here to bring you back home."

Spots stopped his panicked race. The sound of Eric's reassuring voice seemed to soothe him. His large ears rose high on top of his head. His white tail flicked alertly.

The group approached, slow and cautious. Instinctively, they fanned out into a semicircle around the little deer.

Suddenly, a cold wind blew, rattling the trees. Spots lifted his head higher, almost as if the wind had carried some scent to him.

Taylor jumped back, startled as Spots abruptly took a quick sprint. And then, lifting his front legs, he sailed over the pasture fence.

Instantly, Travis threw himself on the gate, yanking it open. The group ran into the pasture, but Spots dashed into the woods. Before they knew it, Spots was out of sight.

"We have to find him!" Taylor cried.

"But how?" Travis asked, still holding his thumb. "Deer are way faster than we are!"

Eric craned his neck, still looking around. "Well, maybe it was time for Spots to go, anyway. I mean, he *was* getting pretty big. He hardly even *had* spots anymore."

It surprised Taylor that Eric was taking this so well. He had spent more time with Spots than any of the rest of them.

Taylor wished she could feel as accepting as Eric seemed to be, but her stomach was in a knot of worry. Recalling what Claire had said just made her all the more nervous. "But Spots can't survive on his own! Claire told me that the other day. He's never learned how. We've had him for too long."

The group exchanged anxious looks as they began to make their way back to the barn. Mercedes chewed her lip for several minutes before speaking. "Let's all tack up and go look for Spots. Travis, since you don't ride, you can stay here in case Spots comes back."

"But how will you catch him?" Travis asked.

There was a pause. How would they manage this?

"Did I ever tell you guys I know how to lasso?" Mercedes said.

Everyone stopped walking and stared at her incredulously.

"I spent a summer at my uncle's ranch in Texas, helping him with the cattle," she explained with a shrug, as if it was no big deal. "He taught me and I got pretty good."

Chapter 5

When the group reached the barn, they saw Mrs. LeFleur talking to Plum, who hadn't moved from her tack-cleaning station. The barn's owner was a short woman in her early sixties. She had a mop of short, curly brown hair and wore very thick eyeglasses. Today she'd thrown a heavy plaid scarf over her usual barn jacket and had on a pair of work gloves.

"Mrs. LeFleur!" Mercedes called as soon as they were within earshot. "Spots jumped the fence and is missing! We're going to go ride after him and try to find him."

Mrs. LeFleur nodded. "Plum told me. You have my permission; just be careful. Bring phones with you. The last thing I need is for Spots *and* you all to go missing."

"You should come with us," Eric suggested to the ranch owner. "You know the area better than we do." He was right. Taylor remembered that Mrs. LeFleur had spent her childhood right here where the ranch was.

Mrs. LeFleur shook her head quickly back and forth, making her thick-framed glasses wiggle on her face. "No, no, that's all right. I'll stay here and see if Spots comes back. I have paperwork to do."

Taylor was about to press her to come with them but remembered that Mrs. LeFleur didn't ride anymore, despite the fact that she loved horses. Taylor had suspected for a while that it had something to do with Jim LeFleur's accident.

Taylor's father, who had known Mrs. LeFleur and Jim, her son, when he was a boy, told Taylor that he'd never seen Mrs. LeFleur — who had once been a prize-winning jumper — on a horse again after that day.

"Plum, what about you? Could you get Shafir ready and come with us?" Eric asked, looking down at his cousin.

Plum just kept polishing her saddle, not looking up as she shook her blonde head. "No, thanks."

"But Spots can't survive on his own. We could use an extra set of eyes," Taylor said. Her worry about Spots overruled her dislike of asking Plum for anything.

"I said no, *thanks*," Plum sneered, looking up at the group with a glare. She began polishing her stirrup leathers and added, "I have work to do here. And you're never going to find that deer."

"Whatever, that's fine," Mercedes said, taking charge of the group once again. "We're wasting time. Come on, let's go."

Mercedes, Taylor, and Eric hurried to get their horses, quickly grooming and tacking them. Within ten minutes they were mounted and ready.

Mercedes, on Monty, was the first one outside the stable. When Taylor rode Prince Albert out, Mercedes was already practicing lassoing a fence post. She would raise the lasso above her head, twirl it around a few times, and then send the rope flying through the air to land with the post in its center.

"I'll lead, since I have the lasso," she said, walking Monty forward, lifting up the lasso and freeing the post. Eric, mounted on Jojo, and Taylor nodded.

"Be careful, you three!" Mrs. LeFleur called after them. "Don't do anything foolish!"

"We won't!" Taylor called back, watching for a moment as Mrs. LeFleur pursed her lips and straightened her glasses, then headed back into the office.

The three riders cut through the upper pasture and into the woods in the direction they had last seen Spots. The cold, fallen leaves crunched beneath the horses' hooves as they made their way along the winding trails. Taylor zipped up her jacket — it was even colder in the woods since the sun couldn't shine through the thick trees. She squinted through the slanting shadows, trying to look for signs of Spots. Deer blended in almost seamlessly into the woods, which was perfect to protect them from predators, making it hard to find their tan hides among the brush.

After more than an hour of squinting, straining, and huffing and puffing up and down the wooded hills, Taylor was beginning to lose hope.

Eric looked around and sighed. "Hey, guys, it's getting dark. We should probably turn ba —"

"Shh! Look!" Mercedes hissed, and pointed to a small clump of brown fur about fifty feet away from them.

The group stopped walking and fell silent, not wanting to scare Spots off. Mercedes pressed her finger to her lips and looked back at Taylor and Eric, who kept quiet and still on their mounts. Mercedes silently readied the lasso in her hand, focusing her eyes on Spots.

Mercedes crept forward with Monty, trying to be as stealthy as possible. The horse let out a low exhale of breath, a stream of white air spluttering from his nostrils. With that, Spots jumped to his feet and stared at the horse, eyes wide and white tail held high. Mercedes and Monty were only about twenty feet from Spots now, and all three of them froze. Mercedes and Spots locked eyes.

"Hyah!" Mercedes shouted suddenly, breaking the standoff, kicking Monty into a canter, and raising the lasso above her head.

Spots turned and leaped off into the deeper woods. Mercedes and Monty galloped after the deer, Mercedes twirling the lasso above her head.

Taylor watched, holding her breath, as Mercedes and Monty thundered down the trail, coming closer and closer to Spots.

Soon Mercedes was right behind the racing deer. With a flick of her wrist she let the lasso fly toward him.

"Darn!" Mercedes shouted, bringing Monty to a halt. Spots had darted off the trail and up a nearby hill at the last moment. Taylor and Eric loped up behind Mercedes. Taylor craned her neck to see what Mercedes had caught.

"No one panic," Mercedes said flatly, with dry humor. "This pine tree is totally under control now."

Taylor looked down to see the lasso firmly holding on to a small evergreen. "We were looking for Spots, not a sapling!" Taylor cried.

"I know!" Mercedes spat back, and then hung her head in disappointment. "I tried," she added weakly.

"Oh, hey, you tried your best," Taylor assured her sincerely. "Really, you were awesome." She'd known Mercedes was an amazing rider, but this display had been more than she'd thought even Mercedes was capable of.

"Maybe Spots will come back to the barn when he gets hungry," Eric suggested, turning Jojo back down the trail.

Taylor nodded in agreement, following after Eric. "I guess that's why no one ever goes deer hunting with a lasso. Too hard."

"No kidding," Mercedes said, coiling her lasso back up and putting it around the horn of her Western saddle. "Steers are a lot bigger, slower, and not usually surrounded by trees."

The search party wound their way through the woods and back to Wildwood Stables. As they got back to the barn, they heard the steady rhythm of a horse being worked at a canter. Taylor noted the three-beat sound of the gait and wondered who would be riding this late into the evening. She turned a corner to see Plum riding Shafir over a jump course of verticals, cross rails, and oxers. The chestnut horse was whizzing around turns and rollbacks, sweating and breathing hard despite the frosty air.

The lights in the ring cast their glow on Plum's determined face as she set her sights on the next jump. Shafir went sailing over an oxer as Plum leaned forward, into two-point, reaching her arms up the horse's neck. As Shafir cleared the jump, she returned to her former position.

Taylor looked at Eric for an explanation. "Why is she working Shafir so hard? It's pretty cold and late for this."

"Plum is determined to win the next competition at Ross River Ranch," Eric said, dismounting Jojo and loosening the cinch. Taylor did the same, bringing Prince Albert's reins over his head.

Taylor's jaw dropped. This was such unexpected news. "But the beginner level is full, I thought," she said, patting Prince Albert on the neck absentmindedly.

"I guess she decided that she's ready to try some of the higher levels, then," Eric replied with a shrug.

"What? Really? But she knows *I'm* trying the harder levels!" Taylor exclaimed, suddenly much more nervous about the tougher competition.

Eric turned and looked at Taylor. "You know Plum shouldn't have even been in that lower level during the last show, right? And you beat her then, so why are you worried? Really, though, I don't think Plum even cares that you'll be there."

Or does she? Taylor thought. *Maybe she does care . . . about not letting me win again.*

Chapter 6

On Friday, after school, Taylor rode her bike down Wildwood Lane and for the first time noticed that the evergreen trees seemed more prominent than before. The towering pines now stood out among the other leafless trees and kept the area from looking too barren. But they were a reminder that the official start of winter was only a few weeks away.

Taylor came to the sign that marked the entrance to Wildwood Stables. Someone — probably Mrs. LeFleur — had wrapped a spray of holly around the chain that held the sign that announced:

WILDWOOD STABLES

HOME OF HAPPY HORSES AND PONIES

ALL EQUINE LOVERS WELCOME!

Horses Boarded * Riding Lessons * Trail Rides Available

Taylor fought the urge she felt each time she read this sign, which was often. She always wanted to take a permanent marker and add on a last line that said: *The Best Place on Earth.*

It was what she truly felt about Wildwood. The ranch was a special place where only good things happened. Where else could a homeless horse and pony like Prince Albert and Pixie be taken in and treated so well? And at what other horse ranch could a girl like Taylor, whose family didn't have a lot of money, have her own horse and learn to ride and jump for free? Wildwood had even made it possible for her to win the lessons with the renowned Keith Hobbes.

Wildwood Stables was really a magical spot.

Taylor started pedaling again, feeling lucky to have arrived at her favorite place in the world. But her mood darkened when she saw a one-horse trailer parked in front of the main building. Taylor recognized the car it was hitched to. It belonged to Daphne's father. The back door of the trailer was open, and the loading ramp was out.

Dropping her bike against the bare maple beside the corral, Taylor ran toward the main building. She got there just as Daphne was leading Mandy from the stable.

Taylor had known this was coming, but somehow she'd never really believed it would happen. Seeing Mandy actually leaving was more than Taylor could stand.

"You're not really taking her, are you?" Taylor blurted breathlessly.

"I told you I was going to," Daphne reminded her, a note of apology in her voice. "You knew that."

"I didn't know it was definite!" Taylor countered.

"I told you," Daphne insisted.

Daphne kept leading Mandy toward the back of the trailer.

"You can't do this, Daphne," Taylor persisted, walking alongside her. "You've been part of Wildwood from the very beginning. You love the place as much as I do. How can you leave?"

61

"They're offering Mandy free board, Taylor. Free board at Ross River Ranch! You know what the place looks like. How can I say no to that?"

Taylor stopped and folded her arms. "You're not loyal," she said.

Daphne halted Mandy. "Don't say that, Taylor. This is a once-in-a-lifetime chance for me."

"*This*, right here, is a once-in-a-lifetime chance," Taylor argued. She spread her arms wide as if to gather all of Wildwood in her embrace. "*This* is the special place. There are a ton of other places like Ross River, where people who are lucky enough to be rich can have the best of everything for their horses. But this is the place that *we* helped Mrs. LeFleur build — you, me, Mercedes, and Travis. *We* made this happen! How can you leave it?"

"I have the chance to work with Keith Hobbes," Daphne said softly. With her head down, she moved onto the back of the trailer and began to walk Mandy up the ramp.

Taylor watched Mandy halt on the ramp. Her gray ears twitched. Did she know she was leaving this place forever? Did she understand she'd no longer live across from Prince Albert and Pixie, or next to Cody, the Colorado Ranger gelding who was her neighbor in the stall next door? Taylor knew that horses were like humans in that they formed relationships and emotional attachments with other horses, as well as with people.

Daphne clicked for Mandy to keep moving into the trailer, and her horse obeyed. In the next minute, Daphne was pulling the ramp away.

Daphne's father walked out of the main building beside Mrs. LeFleur. They shook hands, and Mr. Chang headed to his car.

Taylor looked to Mrs. LeFleur imploringly. She wanted to cry out — *Do something!* But Mrs. LeFleur hadn't noticed her. The ranch owner walked behind the Changs' car and helped Daphne lock the trailer door. They hugged, and Daphne ran up to the car to join her father.

Taylor stood beside Mrs. LeFleur, and together they watched the trailer pull out, Daphne's hand waving from the window. "Do you think we'll ever see them again?" Taylor asked.

Mrs. LeFleur poked Taylor's arm sharply. "You'll be in high school with Daphne next year, silly girl. And don't you take lessons over at Ross River Ranch? Of course you'll see her."

Taylor sighed. "It won't be the same. And I only have one more lesson left at Ross River."

This seemed to surprise Mrs. LeFleur. "Only one left?" she repeated sympathetically. "My, that went fast."

"It did," Taylor agreed, nodding.

Mrs. LeFleur studied Taylor a moment. "Then you'll just have to win some more, won't you?"

Mrs. LeFleur made it sound so simple. Taylor wished it seemed that easy to her. To Taylor, the fact that she'd won the first set was a piece of great luck that she could never hope to reproduce again — especially not when she'd be riding in the next level of competition.

Mercedes came to join them. "All the horses have been fed and watered," she reported. "Taylor, could you help me muck some stalls?"

"Sure," Taylor agreed. "Daphne just left with Mandy."

Mercedes wiped a dark curl from her forehead. "I know. I didn't want to come out to watch them drive off. I couldn't take it. Who's going to give lessons now?"

"I've been thinking about that," Mrs. LeFleur replied. "How about you?"

"Me?" Mercedes cried, pretending to be shocked.

Taylor bit down on a smile. Mercedes was not one bit surprised by this. Taylor knew Mercedes was dying to give lessons. She was always looking for the chance to instruct riders who came to the stable just to ride, especially the younger ones.

"I'm sure I could do it," Mercedes said. "You know I've been riding since I was six, and I've had great instructors. You can see what an amazing horse Monty is. I trained him myself, and not many other girls my age could have —"

"Oh, I know you're a wonderful rider," Mrs. LeFleur cut Mercedes off. "You're one of the best. I think both of you will make terrific instructors."

"Me?" Taylor asked with a gasp. Unlike Mercedes, Taylor was genuinely shocked by Mrs. LeFleur's suggestion.

"Taylor?" Mercedes cried at the same time.

Mrs. LeFleur was amused by their surprise. "Yes, Taylor. I've had a number of inquiries from the parents of children as young as five who are total beginners and are looking for lessons. I think you'd be wonderful with them, Taylor. You could use Pixie for the very little ones. And Prince Albert has become so wonderfully sensible and steady with slightly older children. Mercedes could instruct the somewhat more advanced riders."

Taylor was dumbstruck by this idea. Could she really be a riding instructor?

Mercedes scowled. "Isn't Taylor sort of uh . . . uh . . . *new* to horseback riding?"

"She certainly knows the basics well enough to teach them," Mrs. LeFleur replied. "And she's gotten some experience from helping out with the volunteer programs we've had here, and the children's parties."

Was it true? Taylor wondered if she really did know enough to be a teacher. Mrs. LeFleur wouldn't let her try it if she didn't truly think so.

Taylor discovered she was smiling, though she hadn't realized it. Taylor Henry, Riding Instructor. Cool.

Turning toward Mercedes, Taylor was about to say it would be fun for them to both be riding instructors together. But all she saw was Mercedes' back as the girl walked away.

"Is she mad because I'm going to teach, too?" Taylor asked Mrs. LeFleur, intuitively guessing what was bothering Mercedes.

Mrs. LeFleur shrugged. "Don't worry about it. Mercedes has to learn that she can't always be the big cheese around here."

Taylor nodded, but she felt uneasy. What was happening at Wildwood? First, Daphne had left, and now Mercedes was miffed at her. Even Spots had leaped away.

Chapter 7

Taylor sat in the heated office at Wildwood, flipping through one of Mrs. LeFleur's old books. Its yellowed pages showed different gymkhana patterns and games. Some of them looked fun — definitely something she could do with her lesson group.

The door creaked open and a blast of cold air made Taylor look up to see who had entered the office. Mercedes bustled in, looking hurried. Her curly hair was piled underneath a blue ski cap.

"What are you doing? Come on, the kids will be here soon!" Mercedes said as she grabbed a clipboard from near the computer.

"Just looking up some things to try with the beginners," Taylor said, shutting the book and placing it back on the shelf. "This book has lots of horse games and contests. I read the book's introduction, and it said that here in the northeast we call it gymkhana, but out west they use the Native American name for it, which is O-Mok-See, which just means games on horseback. But don't you think it sounds much cooler and —"

"Whatever! We don't have time for this!" Mercedes exploded.

Taylor felt stung by her impatience. "It's only three-thirty. The kids won't be here until four."

Mercedes looked at Taylor as if she had just spoken in Latin. "Seriously?" she asked, her tone implying irritation rather than confusion. "You have to go get your horses ready."

Taylor hesitated before she said, "Well, I was thinking the kids would learn more about grooming and tacking if I taught them how, instead of me just getting the horses ready for them."

Mercedes waved her right hand dismissively in Taylor's direction. "Whatever. You can do what you want. *I'm* going to go get *my* horses ready so that the kids will have plenty of riding time. See you out there."

Taylor stood up as Mercedes walked out of the office door into the chilly December air. Now unsure what she should do, Taylor paused, rethinking her plans. She decided to go ask Mrs. LeFleur, who was outside talking to a prospective boarder.

Walking up cautiously, she asked quietly, "Uh, Mrs. LeFleur? Sorry to interrupt, but do you think it's okay, for the first couple of lessons, that I teach the kids how to groom and tack *before* they start riding?"

Mrs. LeFleur looked at Taylor and smiled encouragingly. "I think that's a great idea, especially since you're teaching the beginner class. It's important that they get the basics."

Taylor nodded and took a deep breath. Mrs. LeFleur looked into Taylor's eyes, as if she could see the worry there. "Relax," she reassured her, lowering her voice and putting her face closer to Taylor's. "You'll be fine, and if you need help I'll be right here, talking with Mr. Segarra."

Mr. Segarra gave a smile, extending his hand. "Pleased to meet you. My daughter, Roberta, is starting lessons today. With the older kids, I believe. We're thinking about bringing our horse down for boarding as well," he explained.

Taylor shook his strong, rough hand. He wore jeans with white paint splotches on them and a red and gold plaid shirt. By his look she guessed he was in construction. "Nice to meet you, too," Taylor said. "I'm going to be teaching the younger group today. Real beginners."

Mr. Segarra chuckled knowingly. "I remember my first time on a horse. The darn thing spooked at something and bolted. I was so scared, it practically turned my hair straight!" He laughed, running a calloused hand through his thick, curly hair for emphasis.

Taylor smiled and said, "I know how scary that can be. I got bucked off of my friend Eric's horse not too long ago."

"Didn't stop me from getting right back on, though," Mr. Segarra said, scratching at his stubbly beard. "And you either, hmm?"

"Nope," Taylor said with a grin. "Always have to get back in the saddle." Feeling more confident now, and knowing that Mrs. LeFleur would be nearby if anything were to go wrong, Taylor waved good-bye to the two adults. "Nice to meet you, Mr. Segarra. I'm going to go pull the grooming buckets and tack I need. Talk to you all later!"

Taylor headed toward the tack room, passing Mercedes, who was frantically tacking up four horses — Cody, Jojo, Forest, and Monty — in the aisle. She wondered if she should ask Mercedes if she needed any help, but knowing how independent and, at the moment, high-strung Mercedes could be, decided against it.

Taylor brought three grooming totes, saddles, pads, and bridles into the aisle before approaching Prince Albert's stall. Coming up to the black horse, she grabbed his halter from the door. She slid the stall door open and gently clucked at Prince Albert, trying to get his attention.

"Ready to help with a demonstration, boy?" she asked, petting the horse softly on his neck and sliding the halter over his ears.

Prince Albert's ears pricked forward, interested. He neighed, as he always did when spoken to. Taylor loved this about him, although she loved almost everything about him. It made her feel like he was answering her.

From the next stall Pixie whinnied, as if to ask, "Me, too?"

"Not today, girl," Taylor replied in a friendly tone. "But if I have any really little kids you might be just the right size. I won't know until they get here, though."

Taylor stepped around to Pixie's stall to pet her frizzy blonde forelock. "I bet they'll all love you and want to bring you treats. You're such a pretty girl." Pixie dipped her head, allowing Taylor to scratch gently between her ears.

It was just around four when the kids started to arrive. Some came in pairs, others alone. Most of the parents stayed to watch, while a few dropped off their child with a peck on the cheek and a "Have fun!"

Mercedes had brought the four horses into the front riding ring and called out to the forming group, "If you are with the advanced, older group, come here!" A few of the taller children glanced at each other, unsure, and walked forward. Some of their parents followed, while others stayed and chatted with one another.

Taylor came out from the back of the barn, Prince Albert in tow. She spoke to the group of youngest kids — two girls and boy. The oldest-looking girl appeared to be about seven. Taylor guessed that the boy and girl were five or six.

She would need Pixie, after all. And Taylor was glad Mercedes hadn't used Shafir. The young mare was relatively small compared to the other horses.

"Hi, everyone. I'm Taylor, and this is my horse, Prince Albert." She gestured to Prince Albert, who had lowered his head to nibble on what was left of a fuzzy dandelion. "If you're in the beginner group, which I guess you are," she continued, motioning toward the three remaining kids, "you can come on over here. I'm going to show you a couple of things before we get you on. Parents, you're welcome to come along if you want."

The children were shooed forward by their parents, a few of them casting cautious glances over their shoulder as they moved toward Taylor. Taylor bent forward as they came closer to get on their level.

"Hi, there. Again, you can call me Taylor, and this is Prince Albert. What are your names?" she asked, trying to sound as friendly as possible.

"My name is Katlyn Rumbold!" The smallest girl, a brunette dressed in jeans and pink cowboy boots spoke up first, jerking a thumb toward her chest for further indication. The little girl turned and looked at the boy next to her, giving him a sharp poke in the arm and demanding, "Say your name!"

"I'm Ad —" the little boy started to say, very quietly.

"His name is Adam!" said Katlyn, cutting him off. "He's my twin brother, but he's really quiet."

Taylor laughed. "Well, nice to meet you both. And what's your name?" she asked, turning to the remaining girl.

"Sarah," the girl said, twisting her ponytail around her fingers. "Can I pet your horse?"

"Sure!" Taylor said, standing up and tugging Prince Albert forward. "In fact, can you guys help me get Prince Albert ready to ride? I sure could use the help. And then, once we learn how to get him ready, we can get *your* horses ready and go ride!"

Katlyn cheered and jumped up, while Adam gave a small smile and nodded. Sarah reached forward and gently patted Prince Albert's muzzle as the horse finished off the remains of more dandelions.

Taylor reached into the grooming tote, pulling out a currycomb. "Can anyone tell me what this is used for?"

"For cleaning the mane?" Adam asked quietly.

"No, silly!" shouted Katlyn, slugging her brother in the arm. "It's for brushing the horse's body, duh!"

Taylor chuckled. "No hitting, please. And you're both close. We use this currycomb to scrub any caked-on dirt or extra hair off the horse's body. Here, watch me, and then you all can try."

Taylor demonstrated how to curry, scrubbing small circles around the mass of Prince Albert's body. She then had the children practice on different sections of Prince

Albert. Taylor silently reminded herself to get something good for him for Christmas — she was so lucky he put up with the children's shouting and quick motions. She went through all of the grooming and then tacking, making sure to focus on things such as saddle pad placement and how to tie in horse gear.

"All right!" Taylor declared after the last child had practiced. "Let's go get *your* horses ready to go ride!"

"Yeah!" Katlyn cheered as she pumped a small fist in the air. The other two children nodded enthusiastically.

As Taylor led the group into the barn, she glanced over her shoulder toward the ring to see how Mercedes was doing. Although she couldn't hear exactly what Mercedes was saying, she could guess. Mercedes shouted something to one of her riders, then paused and shouted it again. She then stormed over to the student and made a quick, frustrated motion. The horse side-stepped away from the flailing hand, and the rider clutched hold of the saddle horn.

Wondering what was going on in the ring, Taylor turned back to her group of small children. Although it required a lot of patience and repetition, she enjoyed working with the kids. Their, or at least Katlyn's, enthusiasm was contagious, and Taylor couldn't help but grin as she helped them tack up and head into the ring.

The children all giggled as Taylor had them play games like Simon Says and Red Light, Green Light on their horses and pony. Although they were only able to go at a walk, it was still fun to watch them try to tag her during a game of Slow-Motion Tag.

Taylor discovered that she enjoyed teaching with games. The kids were learning control and balance without even realizing it. Before she knew it, it was time for them to dismount. She went around to each of them, helping them slide their leg behind them and then lowering them to the ground.

As Taylor led them back to the barn to untack, she heard Mr. Segarra talking to someone.

"But I don't *want* to come back!" complained a slim brunette girl whom Taylor presumed to be his daughter, Roberta.

"Well, the board here is pretty cheap, and you can take discounted lessons," Mr. Segarra countered, crossing his arms over his chest.

"Fine, we can board Chester, but I *do not* want to take lessons here," Roberta said.

"Why not? Was it that bad?" Mr. Segarra asked, brows furrowed.

"My instructor was so *mean*! She yelled at me for picking up the wrong lead. I don't even know what that means!" Roberta cried, taking off her helmet.

Mr. Segarra sighed and said, "All right. I guess we can look for someplace else, then."

"Or maybe that other girl can teach me," Roberta said, pointing to Taylor. "They looked like they were having fun over there."

Taylor's brows shot up in surprise. *Me? But that girl is only a few years younger than me.* Just then, out of the corner of her eye, she could see Mercedes come storming toward them, heading to the office. She had clearly heard what Roberta said, as had everyone else in front of the barn.

Her dark brown eyes fixed on the office door, Mercedes breezed past Taylor. Taylor opened her mouth to say something comforting as Mercedes walked by but couldn't get anything out before Mercedes had wheeled on her heel, spinning to face Taylor. Pointing a finger in Taylor's face, she said, "Just don't say anything, okay? I don't even have *time* to be teaching. I should be out practicing for the show. And so should *you*, not that it will matter. You're still going to get your butt handed to you by Plum. At least she can *afford* lessons with Keith Hobbes, even if she doesn't win."

Taylor's mouth hung open as Mercedes stormed into the office. It felt as though someone had thrust a knife into her chest and twisted it. Tears of pain, betrayal, and embarrassment sprang to Taylor's eyes. Swallowing the growing lump in her throat, Taylor took a wavering breath to calm her nerves.

A small tug on her sweatshirt made Taylor jump. She looked down to see Adam, his big blue eyes gazing up at her.

"You okay?" he asked quietly, staring into Taylor's water-filled eyes.

Taylor took another steadying breath and managed a smile, patting Adam on the head. "Yeah, I'm great, buddy. Thanks for asking. Let's go put away your horse, okay?"

Taylor let Sarah take Prince Albert's lead to walk him to his stall. She stayed close to the twins as Adam took Shafir and Katlyn led Pixie in.

"Did you guys have fun?" Taylor asked them.

"Yeah!" the three children responded together.

"Good! That's what counts," Taylor told them. It's what she had always believed. It was too bad Mercedes couldn't see it that way.

Chapter 8

When Eric and Plum pulled up in Plum's mother's black SUV, Taylor was even happier than usual to see Eric. His presence meant she wouldn't have to be alone with Mercedes in the barn.

Eric got out of the car and went to the backseat, where he took out a plastic grocery bag. "Hey, how did your first lesson go?" he asked Taylor as he shut the car door behind him.

"*You're* giving lessons?" Plum questioned disdainfully. "*You?*"

Taylor ignored Plum's shocked and derisive tone. "Uh-huh," was all she said. Why was everyone so upset about her being an instructor? Turning her attention back to Eric, she smiled. "The lesson went really well, I think. The kids seemed happy, anyway, and I know they learned a lot."

Plum rolled her eyes. "I give up. Taylor Henry giving horseback riding lessons. What's next?" Shaking her head in exaggerated bewilderment, Plum headed into the main building.

"Don't mind her," Eric apologized for his cousin. "I think it's great that you're teaching. Are you getting paid?"

Taylor nodded happily. "Mrs. LeFleur takes half the price of the lesson, and she gives me half. It's the same thing she did with Daphne. I'm so glad I'll be making some money. There are so many things I want to get for Pixie and Prince Albert."

"I know you want to get blankets for them."

"That will be the first thing. Horse blankets are so expensive, though. I hope I can save enough money before it gets too cold."

An icy wind shook the branches of the bare trees, as if

to underline Taylor's concern with an example of how bad the weather could get. Folding her arms, Taylor shivered. "And it hasn't even snowed yet," she added. "Are you going to take Jojo out for a ride?"

"Later, I hope." Eric reached into his plastic bag and took out a white block about the size of a brick. "It's a salt lick," he explained. "I want to put it up in the pasture. You're really not supposed to feed deer in the winter. It causes all sorts of problems. It encourages lots of deer to hang out in one area, which isn't good, for one thing."

"Then why do you want to do it?" Taylor asked.

Eric studied the label wrapped around the white block. "This block isn't too bad. It's fortified with minerals and apple juice. I'm not going to leave it out there all winter. I just want to see if I can lure Spots back with it. I read an article online that said baby deer bond with whoever raised them."

"That was mostly you," Taylor said.

"I know," Eric agreed. "That's why I'm hoping that he'll come to me if he's hungry enough." He tossed the salt block from hand to hand. "It probably won't work."

"It's worth a try," Taylor encouraged him.

"Come on," Eric said. "We'll go now."

Prince Albert was still saddled from the lesson. Eric quickly tacked up Jojo, and together they walked the horses toward the upper pasture. "How are you doing with your jumping?" Eric asked as they traveled side by side.

"Keith has taught me a lot. I have one more lesson with him. He says we'll only jump. I'm still knocking over rails left and right. I don't know if I'll be ready for the competition."

"I can work with you this afternoon, if you'd like," Eric offered.

"That would be so great!" Taylor cried. "Are you sure you have the time?"

"Sure."

"But what about Plum? I'm competing against her, and she doesn't care who wins, as long as it's not me."

Eric wrinkled his forehead in a skeptical expression. "Do you think she's really that set against you?"

"Yes," Taylor insisted. "Why else was she competing at the beginner level when I was a beginner? Now that I'm moving up, she's moving up. Don't you find that odd?"

"I think it's a coincidence," Eric said evenly.

Taylor didn't want to argue this point anymore. Plum was Eric's cousin, after all. "Maybe it is a coincidence," she conceded, though, in her heart, she didn't believe that for a second.

When they got to the pasture, they dismounted. Eric had brought some wire in his plastic bag, and he used it to fasten the block to one of the fence posts. "I'll sit here for a while every day as quietly as I can and hope Spots shows up," Eric explained. "If I can get a rope around his neck, maybe I can lead him back to the stable."

Once the block was set up, they remounted and sat in their saddles for a while in silence, waiting and hoping, while Jojo and Prince Albert nibbled the grass. Prince Albert sputtered occasionally and looked around, seeming not quite sure what all the waiting was for.

The sky slowly took on a purple tint as the sun dropped lower in the sky. Taylor shivered, gazing at the woods where the trees swayed in the wind. She had serious doubts about the chances of this plan working, but as long as Eric wanted to try it, she'd stick with him.

"If a deer comes out, how will we know it's Spots?" she asked him.

"I'll know," Eric assured her. "I'll just know."

They waited for almost a half hour before Eric suggested they return to the stable.

"We can try again tomorrow," Taylor suggested.

When they were almost in front of the main building, Taylor saw that her mother's car was parked in front. As Taylor led Prince Albert into the main building, past Mrs. LeFleur's office, she looked through the door window into the room. Her mother was inside showing Mrs. LeFleur pictures of the various parties and events she had catered.

"She wants Mrs. LeFleur to hire her for the winter carnival," Taylor explained to Eric, who came alongside her. He was leading Jojo and stopped to peer into the office with Taylor.

"That's going to be fun," Eric commented.

Plum's voice reached them from Shafir's stall. "I know.

I know. You're right. She's so odd." Plum seemed to be on her cell phone with a friend. "Get this . . . they're letting her teach lessons here. Can you believe it? She barely rides herself!"

Taylor tapped Eric's shoulder and pointed toward Shafir's stall — just in case he hadn't realized that Plum was talking about her.

"I know she beat me," Plum continued, "but that was just because this crazy horse I lease is so out of control. The trainers here are so terrible. They let the horse do whatever it wants."

At this, Taylor's jaw dropped, and her eyes went wide with indignation. Daphne and Mercedes had trained Shafir. They'd brought her from being a gorgeous wild creature to an agreeable and responsive tame horse without breaking her spirit — and they'd taken over Shafir's training just so Plum wouldn't ruin her by pressing her too hard and being too harsh.

"Don't worry," Plum told her friend. "I'll beat her this time. I've been working with Shafir day and night. I've got this horse doing exactly what I want this time. I just can't stand a scruffy little nobody like Taylor Henry winning horse events. Horseback riding is for people like us."

Taylor thumped Eric's arm. "See? What did I tell you?"

"Wow," Eric said softly. "I had no idea. Wow."

That night Taylor sat at her kitchen table, still fuming over Plum's words. She stabbed the piece of pot roast on her plate with her fork, flipped it over, and stabbed it again.

Her mother watched her from across the table. "You have to try to forget about it, Taylor. You know how she is."

"A scruffy little nobody," Taylor grumbled. *"A scruffy little nobody."*

"Are you?" Jennifer asked.

"Am I what?"

"A scruffy little nobody."

What was her mother talking about? "Of course not!"

"Well, then."

"Well, what?" Taylor exploded. Did her mother think it was even possible that Plum was right? What was she trying to get at?

"You know it's not true, so don't let it bother you," Jennifer advised.

Taylor considered this for a moment. "Easy for you to say," she grumbled. "Nobody called *you* that."

"How do you think I felt when I got laid off?" Jennifer challenged.

"You were the last hired — so the first fired. Except I know you weren't fired, you were laid off. So that's not like being called a nobody."

"It still made me *feel* like a nobody," Jennifer said. "Don't you think that part of me feels that if they really valued all the hard work I did over there, they never would have let me go?"

"I guess," Taylor replied. She hadn't given it much thought.

"It hurt my feelings," her mother added. "So I know how you feel. But I know I did my best, so I can't let it bother me."

"But it still does bother you," Taylor pointed out. She could tell it did from the look on her mother's face.

Jennifer's face broke into a gentle smile. "It does. I have to admit it."

"See?" Taylor said.

"I know," her mother allowed. "But I'm trying not to let it bother me because I know better. And you should know better, too. If ever there was *anybody* who is not a *nobody* — it's you."

Taylor and her mother stretched across the table and hugged. "Don't let Plum get you down," Jennifer said.

"I won't," Taylor said. "Plum is the pits. Get it? Plum pits?"

Jennifer shoved her playfully. "How about an ice cream soda?" she suggested.

"Great idea!" Taylor cheered. "A root beer float with chocolate ice cream?"

"You got it," Jennifer said, standing.

"So, are you going to cater the winter carnival?" Taylor had been so angry and insulted by Plum that she hadn't even asked.

"No. Mrs. LeFleur said she can't afford a caterer for this event," Jennifer said as she took the ice cream from the freezer. "But she's going to allow me to sell some of my pies and cookies at the carnival and to distribute flyers advertising my business."

"That's almost as good," Taylor commented.

"I think it is," Jennifer agreed.

There was a knock on the side kitchen door, and Claire let herself in. Bunny's toenails clicked across the floor as she scampered in ahead of Claire.

"You're just in time for ice cream floats," Taylor greeted her.

"I've always had excellent timing," Claire joked, sitting at the table. "How did your talk with Mrs. LeFleur go?" she asked Taylor's mom.

"I'll have a booth selling some of my food and advertising."

"Once they taste your cooking, you'll have more business than you can handle," Claire assured her.

"I didn't forget you, either," Jennifer added. "I asked if you could have a spot to try to adopt out some of your stray cats and dogs. Mrs. LeFleur said sure."

"Awesome!" Claire cried happily. "You are the best friend ever. Can you help me with that, Taylor?"

"I'll help you both," Taylor offered. "Though I might have to also do pony rides."

"No problem," Jennifer and Claire said at the same time, which made the three of them laugh. Taylor was feeling much better — and the ice cream soda her mother set in front of her was definitely going to help put her right on track again, too.

Maybe this was the time to ask for the fee money for the Ross River Ranch event.

"You know how I have this job now, giving riding instructions at Wildwood?" Taylor began. "I started today. I get half of whatever Mrs. LeFleur earns on the lesson."

"That's so great!" Claire said enthusiastically.

"I'm proud of you, honey, but how is this going to affect your schoolwork?" Jennifer added cautiously.

"It won't. I promise it won't," Taylor pledged. "The thing is, I'm earning money now, so I'd pay you back." She pulled fifteen dollars from her back pocket. "I earned this today, but . . ."

"You need more than that to enter the Ross River Ranch event," her mom finished her sentence for her. "How much?"

"I need thirty-five more dollars," Taylor revealed sheepishly.

Her mother sat for a moment, her face blank. It was almost as if she hadn't heard Taylor.

Taylor looked to Claire. Was her mother all right?

Claire just held up a finger, indicating that Taylor should wait.

"Yes," Jennifer said at last. "Yes, okay." She got up and went to the kitchen cabinet beside the sink and reached up to the highest shelf. Standing on her toes, she strained to pull out a jar. Unscrewing the lid, she pulled out a twenty, a ten, and a five, and set down the empty jar. "Here you go," she said, handing Taylor the money.

"Thanks, Mom. I'll pay you back. I promise," Taylor said.

Jennifer waved her away. "This one is on me. Save your money, though. After this, you're responsible for your own entry fees."

Taylor got up and gave her mother a quick hug. "I'm going to do my homework right now, so you don't have to worry about that."

"Good girl," her mom said. "And don't get on the phone with Travis."

"I won't, really."

As Taylor hurried from the kitchen she heard her mother and Claire discussing what different foods Jennifer might sell at the winter carnival. Hurrying to her room, she scooped her backpack off the floor and took out her books. She decided to tackle her math homework first, just to get it out of the way before she got too tired.

Two hours later, Taylor yawned widely and shut her earth science textbook. Stretching, she decided to grab a quick snack to eat before going to sleep.

Taylor knew her mother had gone to bed because she'd stopped in to say good night about an hour earlier. The lights were off in the living room, and only the stove light illuminated the kitchen in its soft glow.

Taylor poured Sugar Pops and milk into a bowl. She was sitting down to eat it when she noticed that her mother had left the empty money jar on the counter. She noticed it had a label and got up to see what it said. The words NEW WINTER JACKET SAVINGS were written on a white label.

Quickly picturing the jacket her mother had been wearing since the weather had gotten colder, Taylor realized she'd seen her in that old navy blue pea jacket for as long as she could remember. Had she had the same jacket for *all* of Taylor's life?

Her mother had given her all the money she'd saved toward buying herself a new winter jacket. Her generosity caused a lump to form in Taylor's throat.

Well, it was only a loan, Taylor decided. She would give lessons and pay every bit of it back. She'd be the best horseback instructor anyone had ever seen.

Chapter 9

Great work!" Keith Hobbes praised Taylor from the center of the ring. "You can walk and relax now."

Taylor wiped the sweat from her brow and gave Gracie, the roan horse she was riding, a pat on the neck. English riding was a lot of fun, but also a lot of work! Her thighs burned from posting, both with and without stirrups, and from riding around the ring in two-point.

It was so nice to be able to ride weekly in a heated, indoor ring. Wildwood Stables couldn't afford to heat an indoor ring, let alone construct one.

"So, Taylor," Keith said as she rode by, "this is your last lesson. Will you be coming back after this?"

Taylor chewed on her lip and admitted, "I don't know. The only way I can afford to keep riding here is if I win the next competition. And that's a bit of a stretch."

"So win it," Keith stated matter-of-factly. "Are you saying you're not confident in your riding?"

"Well, not in the higher levels. The jumps are bigger, and the other people in the competition have been doing this way longer than I have."

"What we've been practicing in lessons is what the judges will ask you to do in the ring. There is nothing there that you haven't done here. I think you stand a very good chance of winning, or at the very least placing."

Taylor smiled, happy to hear his encouraging words. "Well, I'll do my best," she said. "I *would* like to win more lessons with you."

"You win my Most Improved in the Shortest Time Award," Keith said with a chuckle. "You had it in you all along. You just needed a chance to let it show."

Taylor beamed, proud he would bestow such an honor

on her, even if it was just in words and not a real award. But her smile faded when Daphne strode into the arena, glossy black hair trailing behind her.

Daphne walked up to Keith, asking, "Did you want Barclay ridden in the Pelham bit or the D ring?"

"Oh, D ring, please. That would suit him best — if we can even get him bridled this time," Keith replied.

"Yeah, he's a bit of a handful," Daphne remarked with a sigh. Before turning, she cast a cautious glance up toward Taylor. "Hey, Taylor."

Taylor gave a short wave, pursed her lips, and nudged Gracie forward into a walk in the opposite direction. Taylor didn't want to feel hurt and betrayed by Daphne, but she just wasn't able to get over it.

Keith's voice snapped her back to attention. "All right, Taylor. I hope I'll see you next week. I have to go work with that new horse, Barclay." He walked purposefully toward the gate. "Keep cooling Gracie down some more before you dismount."

"I will. Thanks for everything — just in case I don't see you next week."

"Start thinking positive thoughts about that competition right now, and I bet you'll do great," Keith replied with a smile.

"See you!" Taylor called out after him. "Thanks again!"

As Taylor walked Gracie around the ring she returned to her thoughts about the situation at Wildwood, her daydreams occasionally floating in the direction of Eric. Although she didn't want to read too far into it, he *did* seem to pay a lot of extra attention to her. Then again, wasn't that what friends did?

After two circles around the ring, Taylor dismounted Gracie, running her stirrups up and bringing the reins forward over the horse's mane. Still thinking about Eric, she walked out of the ring toward where the groom would be waiting to take Gracie to untack and groom her and place her back in her stall. She still marveled at the luxurious novelty of everything at Ross River Ranch.

As she turned the corner into the aisle, Taylor heard a commotion of clattering hooves on the pavement. Peeking her head around the half-open sliding door, she saw a sorrel Arabian pulling back from the cross ties, twisting his head back and forth in a panic to get free. His hooves scrapped against the floor, and Taylor could see his eyes bulging with fear.

"Whoa, boy, easy!" Keith tried to soothe the horse, moving slowly toward the animal's head, trying to unlatch him from the cross ties. Taylor was intrigued but realized she was still holding on to Gracie's reins.

There was no groom in attendance, and Taylor didn't want to wait for one to arrive as she would have ordinarily done. Instead, she hurried to Gracie's stall, untacked her, and tossed Gracie's blanket on her before rushing back to see what progress Keith had made with the tense Arabian.

Taylor ran toward the aisle and came to a skidding stop, dirt flying up around her. The aisle was silent, and all that remained was the evidence of a battle. Buckets had been knocked over, the bridle lay in a pile, and there were skid marks on the pavement from where the horse's shoes had scraped the floor.

Taylor's breath caught in her throat. *Where was everyone? Were they okay?* She didn't know what to do next.

Suddenly, someone shouted words she couldn't quite

understand. The voice came from the direction of the arena she had just been riding in. Dashing in that direction, she nearly tripped over the barn cat that was sleeping in a tight ball in the center of the walkway.

"Sorry, Stella!" Taylor cried to the cat as she bolted away from her thundering awakening.

Taylor's heart pounded as she came to a stop in front of the ring. No one was in the main riding arena, but when she looked to her left, she noticed the same sorrel horse in the metal round pen nearby, bucking and rearing. Three people stood outside the ring, watching the horse flail its body in the air.

Taylor then realized that only *two* of the people were standing, and one was sitting. *Who would be sitting near a ring with a crazy horse?* she wondered. But in just a few steps more she was able to see that those standing were Keith and Daphne. And then she realized why the third person was sitting — it was Jim LeFleur, of course, in his wheelchair.

Taylor crept up toward the round pen, careful not to interrupt them.

"Thanks, Jim, we really appreciate you coming down," Keith said. "This little Arabian has been giving us one heck of a time."

Daphne nodded in agreement, watching the horse kick his hind legs high up into the air, doing what looked to Taylor practically like a handstand.

"Not a problem," said Jim LeFleur, waving his hand dismissively. "I just want to see this horse start behaving."

Keith looked pensively at the horse as it whirled in a sharp circle. "Yeah, me too," he agreed. "A shame he's so crazy, because he has good bloodlines. He'll be worth a pretty penny when we can calm him down."

The horse threw himself in the air with a violent twist.

"*If* we can calm him down," Keith corrected himself.

"Should we Ace him?" Daphne suggested, looking at the two men.

Jim shook his head. "Acepromazine not needed," he said, referring to the horse tranquilizer usually referred to as Ace. "He just needs to communicate with us."

"He's sure *communicating* that he doesn't want us to mess with him," Daphne said, taking a step back from the flailing horse.

"No, he's saying that he's angry right now but will calm down. He can't keep this up forever," Jim said. "He's like a child. We just need to let him throw his tantrum and get some energy out. We can work with him when he's through."

Taylor crept a little closer, interested in Jim LeFleur's calm, collected demeanor. It constantly impressed her how natural Mrs. LeFleur's son was around horses — maybe it was genetic, because Mrs. LeFleur was the same way, even if Taylor had never seen her ride.

The horse's bucking slowed a little. He dropped his head and licked his lips. "There, look," Jim said. "See how he's calming down? He's showing signs of relaxing. Daphne, could you open the gate for me?"

Daphne nodded and reached forward, creaking the metal door open. Taylor's body tensed as Jim wheeled himself through the opening and into the pen.

Why would he shut himself in with a wild horse? It was suicide!

Jim pressed the button on his electric wheelchair to move forward. The whirring noise and the sight of the wheelchair caused the horse to stop and stand still for a moment, deciding if this new thing was going to hurt him or not.

Ears pricked and nostrils flared, the horse stood rigid. Jim proceeded forward into the center of the ring, and with a loud "Hyah!" and a wave of his arms, sent the horse running in circles around the ring again.

Taylor watched in amazement as every time the horse would come to a stop and face him, Jim raised his arms and shouted, "Hyah!" Each shout sent the horse darting to the rail.

"I'm making it so that the horse can only rest when he is paying attention to us," Jim explained. "Daphne, do you want to come in here and help me?"

Daphne nodded enthusiastically. "Sure, I'd love to!"

Taylor felt a light flicker of envy. It must be amazing to work with these people one-on-one. They really knew what they were doing.

The horse slowed down to a walk and then stopped, looking at Daphne and Jim.

"Now, go and try to approach him, nice and steady. Speak low and slow," Jim advised.

Daphne nodded and made her cautious approach, lead line in hand. "Hey, there, buddy," she said in a low, singsong voice. "You're okay, I'm not going to hurt you."

The horse backed up in three quick steps.

"Now get after him. Chase him," Jim called out. "Don't let him rest until he is fully listening to you."

"Hyah!" Daphne shouted, flicking the lead line out at the horse. The sorrel Arabian gave a small rear and galloped off on his previous path around the ring. Once again, after a few laps, the horse came to a stop and looked intently at Daphne. Again, Daphne approached the horse, speaking in low, soft tones.

"Now, slowly reach out and touch him with the lead rope. Show him that you won't hurt him with it. Stroke his neck," Jim instructed. Daphne did as he said, making her moves slow and deliberate. The horse flinched as Daphne gently stroked his neck, but he did not move.

Uh-oh, Taylor thought as she felt a tickle rise in her nose. She thrust her hands up over her mouth, trying to stifle the sneeze.

Ah-ah-AH-CHOO! Taylor couldn't hold back. As soon as the sneeze had escaped, she quickly ducked down to try to hide herself from the Ross River trainers.

"Taylor?" Daphne inquired, turning to look at her from the ring. "What are you doing there?"

Clearly, she had not been as well hidden as she had thought.

"Uh, well, I heard a lot of noise and came to see if everyone was all right, and, I don't know . . . just kind of kept watching," Taylor explained, cheeks flushing red at having been discovered.

"Do you want to come help, too?" Jim asked her.

Taylor's eyes darted back and forth from Daphne to Keith to Jim. "I don't think I know enough about horse training to really be much help," she said as she came forward.

"Not a problem, just do as I say," Jim said with a warm smile. "I remember you from Wildwood, don't I? Weren't you trying to get your horse to accept a new rider that day I was there with Aunt Devon?"

"Yes," Taylor replied, pleased that he remembered her. "You really helped us that day."

"Glad to hear it."

Taylor noticed that he had a slightly crooked smile, just like Mrs. LeFleur's. She glanced at Keith for assurance as she walked up to the gate. He nodded and made a waving motion with his hands, gesturing for her to enter the ring.

As Taylor entered the center of the ring, the Arabian began to bolt around the perimeter. In the same fashion as before, they all waited for the horse to calm down and face them, and then approached.

Daphne quietly handed the lead line to Taylor and gave her a small nudge, speaking quietly. "There, you try now. Try to pet him with the lead line on the neck. If he backs away, chase after him," Daphne said, repeating Jim's advice.

Taylor nodded and slowly advanced toward the horse, just as she had seen Daphne do before. The sorrel stood, rigid and aware, ready to bolt if anything scared him. Reaching a cautious hand forward, she took the lead line and stroked his neck with it, speaking slowly. "There you go, boy. Are you going to behave now for Jim, Keith, and Daphne? I bet they'd appreciate it." Taylor gently massaged just below his mane with the navy blue cotton rope.

The three watching all looked at each other with approving smiles, and then back to Taylor, who was stroking the horse's muzzle with her palm.

"You're really good with him," Daphne praised.

"Thanks!" Taylor said with a grin. "It's so cool that you get to work here and do stuff like this."

Daphne nodded slowly, a smile spreading across her face. "It really is," she said. "You would love it. I've already learned so much."

"I can tell. Even if I don't win this upcoming competition, I'll have to come visit you here more often," Taylor said, transfixed by the increasingly calm Arabian.

"Totally!" Daphne agreed happily.

"Or you could come visit Wildwood again," Taylor ventured, wondering if Daphne actually would.

Daphne nodded assuredly. "Of course I will. That place is my home. I could never leave it for good."

Taylor smiled broadly, happy to hear Daphne say those words. If Wildwood was Daphne's home, too, that made them family. And that is exactly how Taylor felt about most people there — although she might not get along with everyone all the time, they were a tight-knit group.

Of course, that didn't mean she didn't want to beat some of them, or namely just one person, at her own English riding game.

Chapter 10

Taylor marveled that she had been awake for almost nine hours already, and it was still before noon. Plum, Mercedes, Mrs. LeFleur, and Taylor had been up and busy getting the horses ready before the sun peeked its golden rays over Pheasant Valley. Although Taylor was not a morning person, the thrill of the upcoming competition had knocked any sleepiness out of her. All she felt was excitement.

It had been so hectic, cold, and dark at the barn that morning. They had to do all the morning chores and then groom the horses once more. Taylor was thankful that their manes had already been braided and bundled the night before. When that was finished, they loaded the horses onto Mrs. LeFleur's old trailer and headed over to Ross River Ranch.

Mercedes hardly spoke to Taylor all morning, working in silence. Taylor felt more angry than hurt. She hadn't done anything to Mercedes. Mercedes was jealous that Taylor was the more popular teacher, but that wasn't Taylor's fault. In Taylor's opinion Mercedes was acting like a brat. In the past, Taylor had forgiven Mercedes for her bossy ways and impatient manner, but this was just too much.

Taylor was so angry at Mercedes that she was relieved when the girl announced that her mother would be driving her over to Ross River. "There's just no room in the trailer," she said. At another time, Taylor would have begged Mercedes and Mrs. Gonzalez for a ride. Being crammed in the front seat of the trailer with Plum was not her idea of a good time. But under the circumstances, being stuck in the car with Mercedes would have been even worse.

As Mrs. LeFleur drove up Wildwood Lane and out onto Quail Ridge Road, Plum held her body tight, folding her arms so that no part of her would touch Taylor, who sat beside her. That was completely fine with Taylor. All the way across Pheasant Valley, Plum complained about being embarrassed by the rust stains on the outside of the trailer. Mrs. LeFleur seemed too focused on the upcoming competition, or maybe she was just too sleepy, to pay much attention to her. Taylor did her best to tune Plum out, too. When they finally pulled up the drive to Ross River Ranch and parked, Taylor nearly leaped from the front seat, unable to get away from Plum quickly enough.

The indoor ring at Ross River Ranch had been transformed; it had been cut in half with movable plywood borders. A gleaming white jump course decorated the right half, while the left half was clear and open for equitation classes and schooling.

Taylor enjoyed the ranch's holiday spirit as she walked her course pattern with Plum and Mercedes, noting how each jump had a different seasonal theme. A line of tiny plastic snowmen waved from beneath a vertical, and two small evergreens frosted with fake snow stood proudly on either side of an oxer.

In keeping with the luxurious details at Ross River, each participating horse got its own indoor stall. The horse's name was printed on a small certificate and posted upon the door. Taylor was thankful that Prince Albert would get to be warm and toasty, just like she was, and not out in the cold trailer.

"Hey, big Jacques," Taylor greeted the Percheron as she led Prince Albert past in search of the stable assigned to him. "Hi, Serafina!" she called when she went by her stall.

At the sound of Taylor's voice, Prince Albert whinnied. As always, Taylor pretended he'd actually said something. "Oh, don't be jealous," she scolded with a smile. "These are my new friends, but I still love you the most."

Taylor sat outside Prince Albert's stall, picking nervously at a thumbnail. She thought of how Plum had entered an equitation class earlier that morning and had placed second. Mercedes and Taylor were still waiting for their class to come up. It had cost too much for either of them to enter more than one class.

Taylor's stomach knotted up every time she realized

that she had only one chance to perform perfectly, and that she would be competing against a slew of much more experienced riders. But even if she didn't win, it had been a lot of fun trying the new, harder jumps during practice. The higher level of difficulty pushed her to try new things, which was a plus.

"Hey, what're you doing there?" asked a familiar voice. Taylor gave a small jump of surprise and looked up to see Daphne standing above her. She looked elegant in polished tall black boots, tan breeches, and a red turtleneck sweater.

"Oh, you scared me!" Taylor cried, but she smiled, too. "I'm just thinking about the jump class I'm in. When do you ride?" she asked Daphne, standing up and brushing the dust off of her slightly stained breeches.

"I'm not competing today," Daphne explained. "I'm working. My job is just to help the judge out. Run point cards, walkie-talkie who places to the announcer, give out ribbons, stuff like that."

Taylor chuckled grimly. "Want to put in a good word for me? I could use the help."

"Oh, stop. You'll be great, you always are. Just relax and have a good time. Remember, that's what you're here for: to have fun!"

Taylor nodded in thoughtful agreement. "True. And to win some more lessons!"

"That, too," Daphne agreed. "You'd better start getting Prince Albert ready and warmed up. Advanced Over Fences will be going in three classes. I think Mercedes and Plum are already in the schooling ring."

"That soon? Yeah, I'd better get going," Taylor said, picking up her pad and saddle from the ground where she had been sitting, "Thanks for the heads-up."

"No problem," Daphne replied with a smile. "Keith and I will be watching from the sidelines. See you out there!"

Taylor waved with her free hand and turned to Prince Albert. "You ready to go do some jumps, boy?" she asked as she pulled the door open and started tacking up.

Chapter 11

Time flew by as Taylor tacked and brought Prince Albert out to the schooling ring, where the riders were practicing their jumps. Though intimidated, she got on and rode over a few, trying her best to imagine it was the real thing.

Shoulders back, chin up, heels down, toes up, lean forward, crest release, lean back . . . The words ran through her mind like a meditative chant. Before she knew it, it was time to enter the show ring.

"Advanced Over Fences is on deck. Number 303 will be entering the ring first," the announcer called out over the loudspeaker.

Taylor picked out Mercedes and Plum in the crowd and rode up behind them.

"Number 303, that's you, Plum," Taylor said, looking at Plum's back, where her number was pinned.

"Duh, thanks for the update," Plum responded flatly, not bothering to look at Taylor.

Taylor stuck her tongue out and made a sneering face at Plum's back, putting her gloved hands up to her helmet and wiggling them ... Plum began to turn her head, causing Taylor to drop her hands and look at something decidedly interesting to her side.

The last rider for the previous class exited the ring, and members of the event staff, including Daphne, rushed in to raise the jump rails a few pegs. Taylor gulped at the new height of the jumps and glanced over at Mercedes. Mercedes sat on top of Monty, looking focused and unbothered by the bustle around her.

"Number 303 now entering the ring," the loudspeakers boomed out. Plum tucked her chin and kicked Shafir into a trot, gliding smoothly into the ring.

The crowd watched as Plum directed Shafir through the set of jumps. Riding crop in hand, she cracked Shafir behind her heel, sending the chestnut horse flying forward over a particularly high jump. All of her practice seemed to be proving worthwhile, even if she wasn't a particularly gentle rider. Quick and fluid over the jumps, Taylor couldn't help but be impressed with Plum and Shafir.

"Number 650 is up next, number 518 is on deck," the announcer dictated.

Taylor stretched to get a glimpse of Mercedes' number. A bold black 518 shone from the number card on her back. Taylor began to nudge Prince Albert forward so that she could go say something to her, but it was just a reflex. Remembering their last encounter, Taylor thought better of it and stayed where she was.

A boy on a large buckskin horse was next, number 650. Taylor watched as they raced around the ring, leaping over fences. As the duo approached the last set of jumps, a cross rail to a vertical bounce, the buckskin ducked away from the cross rail, and with a collective gasp from the crowd, the rider went tumbling off the horse's side and crashing into the jump. The buckskin, now free, trotted back to the gate without a rider.

Taylor stood up in her saddle to get a better view of the boy who had fallen. Thankfully, he pulled himself up from the jump, and aside from looking slightly dazed and embarrassed, seemed to be fine. He chased down his horse and got back on, finishing the course and exiting without looking anyone in the eye.

"Penalty," stated the announcer, adding further insult to injury. "Next up is number 518, on deck is number 845."

Taylor recognized her own number, 845. She took a deep breath and left the larger group, following Mercedes toward the gate.

On an impulse, she called out, "Hey, Mercedes."

Mercedes turned around, one eyebrow raised in a questioning manner.

"Good luck," Taylor said.

The corners of Mercedes' lips tugged into a slight smile, her face softening a bit. "You, too," she replied.

"Number 518 now entering the ring," the speakers boomed forth.

Mercedes nudged Monty into a trot as she rode into the ring. Picking up a canter for her courtesy circle, she eased the horse gently from the entry and through the jump course. Taylor marveled at how natural and at ease Mercedes looked in the show ring, as if she had been doing it her whole life. Maybe she had, Taylor realized, up until she'd lost Monty.

Monty sailed with ease over the last set of jumps, and finally the bounce. Taylor exhaled, thankful that her Wildwood coworker hadn't suffered the same fate as the previous rider. The habit of having friendly thoughts toward Mercedes and wishing her well was still with Taylor apparently, no matter how angry Mercedes had made her.

Mercedes exited the ring, giving Taylor an encouraging smile as she passed by.

The announcer boomed out, "Now entering the ring is number 845, on deck is number 113."

Taylor thumped Prince Albert on the neck, "C'mon boy, let's rock this."

His ears perked, Prince Albert nickered as they entered the ring, as if to say, "Everyone watch and learn!"

Taylor, picking up the canter for their courtesy circle, set her eyes on the first jump. They headed toward the cross rail and cleared it without a problem. Eyes trained on her next jump, she turned the corner, and Prince Albert flew over the vertical. The next few jumps went just as smoothly.

As they approached the final set of jumps, the bounce where the boy had fallen, Taylor took a deep breath. She urged Prince Albert into a powerful yet collected canter. They popped up over the first jump, landed, and then lifted upward and over the second jump.

Breathing hard, and thankful they had cleared the jumps, Taylor left the ring and walked Prince Albert back to the large group she had been in before. She looked around and tried to catch Mercedes' eye, but Mercedes was staring straight ahead, back straight, waiting for the other riders to finish and the places to be called. Plum, on the other hand, had taken off her black gloves and was fidgeting with her nails.

As the last few riders finished their course, the tension rose again. It was as though each competitor was holding his or her breath, as if no one in the group was even moving.

"We now have our placing for the Advanced Over Fences class," the announcer said, "with the winner receiving ten free lessons with Ross River Ranch's very own Keith Hobbes."

Taylor glanced over to Keith, who smiled and gave a polite wave to the crowd. Daphne stood next to him, holding the ribbons. She grinned over at Taylor, mouthing "Good job!" to her.

Taylor gave Daphne a thumbs-up and mouthed "Thanks!" back to her.

"In sixth place, we have number 184."

Daphne strode forward, handing a green ribbon to a girl on a palomino horse.

"In fifth place, we have number 113."

Daphne continued en route to a different girl, this one on a dark bay horse, and gave her the pink fifth-place ribbon.

"In fourth place, we have number 845."

Taylor, surprised that she felt truly proud instead of disappointed, smiled as Daphne came up to her, handing her a white ribbon.

"Congrats!" Daphne said, patting Prince Albert on the neck.

"Thanks! It's not first, but that's okay," said Taylor, looking at her new ribbon.

"Hey, it's not last, either! Well done," Daphne said before returning to the center of the ring.

"In third, we have number 303."

Taylor's eyes darted to Plum, who had a smug expression on her face as she accepted the yellow third-place ribbon. *Oh, well,* Taylor thought. *Next time.*

"In second, we have number 788."

Daphne strode over, hooking a red ribbon on a black horse's bridle and extending her congratulations.

"And, finally," the announcer said, making a dramatic pause, "winning first place and ten free lessons with Keith Hobbes is . . ."

Taylor looked around quickly. Mercedes and four other riders were left. It could be any of them!

"Number 518!"

The crowd applauded as Daphne gave a small jump of excitement and headed over to Mercedes. Mercedes thumped Monty on the neck and then pumped her fist in the air.

Daphne handed her the large blue ribbon. Mercedes reached forward and hooked the ribbon on the cheek piece of Monty's bridle.

Her relationship with Mercedes had been rocky, but Taylor couldn't help feeling proud for her fellow Wildwood Stables rider. She clapped enthusiastically with everyone else as Mercedes waved to the crowd.

As the riders dispersed, Daphne walked back over toward Taylor. "Just between you and me," Daphne said, leaning in close, "Keith and I both think you rode better than Plum."

"Then why did she beat me?" Taylor asked, looking over to Plum, who had stuck her ribbon into Shafir's forelock and was making kissy noises at the horse.

Daphne shrugged. "A lot of classes are up to the judge's opinion. It's sort of like gymnastics or figure skating — one judge may like one style of riding, whereas a different judge may like another."

"True. Oh, well, at least someone from Wildwood

won first again. It shows that we're a force to be reckoned with!" Taylor said proudly.

Just then, a whirring noise made Taylor look to her other side. Jim LeFleur was heading over toward where she and Daphne stood talking.

"Great work, kid!" Jim said, smiling proudly up at Taylor.

"Thanks!" she replied, looking back at the jump course she had just completed. "You know, I'm proud I even entered."

"As you should be!" said Jim. "In the words of a fellow rider, John Wayne, 'Courage is being scared to death, but saddling up anyway.'"

Taylor laughed. "Good quote! I like it."

Looking back to where Jim had just come from, Taylor saw Mrs. LeFleur walking up to talk to her riders and congratulate them. The Wildwood owner stopped in her tracks, though, locking eyes with Jim. Taylor looked back and forth between the two, wondering again what exactly it was that had occurred between them so long ago that made them still act this way.

Mrs. LeFleur looked at Taylor, turned, and strode back the way she came. Daphne glanced at Taylor with a worried look, then left and headed toward Mercedes, who was talking to Keith Hobbes at the other end of the ring.

Brow furrowed, Taylor glanced back to Jim.

"Jim, can I ask you a question?" Taylor said quietly.

"Sure, shoot," Jim replied, still looking in the direction of his mother.

"What happened between you and your mother?" Taylor asked.

Chapter 12

Jim LeFleur sighed unhappily. "Are you sure you want to hear this? It's not a real happy story, and you should feel good right now. You did really well out there."

"I'd like to know what happened. I've been wondering about it for a long time," Taylor replied.

Jim moved his wheelchair off to the side so they wouldn't block anyone passing by. Taylor leaned against the wall next to him.

"As you might know, my mom and Aunt Devon are cousins, but they grew up like sisters over at Wildwood Stables. Aunt Devon's parents had a house on the property back then. It was knocked down some years ago."

Taylor recalled seeing the foundation of an old building in the upper pasture. She'd always wondered about it. Now she guessed it must have been where the house had once stood. "I think I know where it is," she said, nodding.

"My dad died in a car accident when I was still a baby, so Mom returned to Wildwood Stables with me to live at the ranch and help run things there."

"What a great place to grow up," Taylor commented.

"It was," Jim agreed. "It was the best place in the world."

Taylor smiled at this. It was funny that he used those exact words. But she didn't want to sidetrack him from his story. She'd been waiting to hear this story for a long time.

"Well, it was around then, when I was twelve or so, that I had the accident that put me in this chair. Mom had taught me to jump. She was such a wonderful horsewoman. Man, you should have seen her go. At competitions, no one could beat her. The only one who ever came close was Aunt Devon, but even she mostly came in second place to my mother."

"I've heard that your mom has lots of ribbons, but she doesn't display them, so I've never seen any," Taylor mentioned.

"Yeah? Who told you that?"

"My dad used to ride down at Wildwood Stables. His name is Steve Henry," Taylor said.

"Get out of here!" Jim cried in astonishment. "You're little Stevie Henry's kid? No way!" He studied her with a sort of wonder. "I do see the resemblance now. Wow! How's he doing?"

"He's good," Taylor said. "So, you were telling me what happened. . . ."

"Okay, so . . . I wanted to compete at a higher level than before, and Mom was nervous about it. I convinced her to work with me, though. We were doing jumps in that corral right in front of the main building. The horse I was on threw a shoe as he was going over a high jump. He knocked over the jump and went down — right on top of me."

Taylor gave a little gasp. She could picture it all perfectly — it must have been so scary and awful at the time.

Jim nodded at her reaction, then continued his story. "Part of my spine was crushed, and I've been in the chair ever since. Mom was so freaked out that she never wanted me to even be near another horse. And as you know, she never rode again, either. We even moved away, down to Bronxville, where Mom still lives."

"But you still loved horses," Taylor said. She could understand that part completely — nothing could make her stop loving horses, either.

"More than anything on Earth," Jim agreed. "But Mom wouldn't budge. After what had happened she wouldn't let me near a barn, let alone a horse. That was where Aunt Devon came in. I convinced her to pick me up in Bronxville and drive me here to Ross River, which she had just opened with her husband. It was only an hour north of Bronxville. I told Mom I was busy with the chess club. For a while she thought I was staying late at school, and that the late bus was dropping me home."

"And did you ride?" Taylor asked.

"I can ride a little if there's someone around strong enough to help me into the saddle. But mostly I just loved being around the horses. I'd sit and watch great coaches like Keith give lessons or train. I learned a lot from hanging around with Enrique and listening to him talk about when he was a horse-racing jockey in Buenos Aires as a young man."

"How did Mrs. LeFleur find out what was going on?" Taylor asked.

Jim laughed lightly. "She found out when she went to school to watch a big chess tournament and discovered that I wasn't even in the chess club. She called Aunt Devon, in a panic that I was missing, and Aunt Devon confessed."

"Was she mad?"

"Mad doesn't even begin to describe it," Jim recalled, shaking his head unhappily. "She called me a sneak and accused Aunt Devon of disrespecting her wishes and lying to her. Aunt Devon tried to apologize, but Mom cut her dead. She hasn't spoken to Aunt Devon in twenty-four years."

"Wow!" Taylor commented. "I guess you missed the horses an awful lot, didn't you?"

"I missed them so much it hurt. I was fifteen years old when Mom found out I was spending time here at Ross

River. I didn't see another horse until I went away to college at eighteen. There was an equestrian team at the college, and my girlfriend at that time rode on it."

"Did Mrs. LeFleur mind that you were spending time with horses again, when you were at school?" Taylor wondered.

"She sure did. She demanded that I stop going to the barn there, but I refused to stop. That's when we had our huge fight. She said she wouldn't pay for my college if I didn't stop going. But I can be just as stubborn as she is, I guess. I dropped out of college, and she and I have been on bad terms ever since."

"What did you do after college?"

"Well, I also started drawing horses at that time, so I kept up with that."

"You're an artist?" Taylor asked, impressed. "Do you sell your work?"

"I've illustrated books and magazines about horses. If you're around, remind me sometime and I'll show you samples of my work. I usually have a sketch pad in the car. I took a job at a horse magazine in their art department, but they moved their offices and I didn't want to move that far away. When I told Aunt Devon I was looking for a job, she offered me one here."

"And I'm so glad I did," said a new voice, behind Taylor.

Taylor turned to see that Devon Ross had been standing in the hallway, listening to their conversation. In her late fifties or early sixties, she was a tall, slim woman. Her dark hair was tied back, as always, in a severe bun. Mrs. Ross carried herself with such poise and dignity that she reminded Taylor of a ballet dancer or even a queen. Taylor had always found her extremely intimidating, but also kind of suspected that she had a soft side. Now, after hearing Jim's story, her suspicion about this was even stronger.

"Aunt Devon, this is —"

Mrs. Ross cut off Jim's introduction. "Taylor and I have met. You were working with your mother at my luncheon a few months ago. We met then."

"That's right," Taylor agreed, a little surprised that the woman remembered.

"Nice riding out there today, young lady," Mrs. Ross asked. "Will you continue to train here with Mr. Hobbes?"

"Thank you, but since I didn't win the prize I can't afford to. My friend Mercedes won, so she'll be coming."

"Ah, yes, the young lady who is currently working Monty for me; she's also a gifted rider."

"Yes, she is," Taylor agreed. "She's so happy to be working with Monty again."

"I'm glad," Mrs. Ross said. She turned her attention to Jim. "Has your mother left the ranch?"

"I presume so. She stormed out in kind of a huff. I don't think she expected to see me here today."

"This has got to end," Mrs. Ross said sadly. "It's been going on for too long."

"You're right," Jim agreed. "I'd be willing to try to straighten things out, but you know how stubborn she is. She feels like we've both betrayed her."

Taylor remembered how hurt she was when she felt Daphne had betrayed her, and her heart went out to Mrs. LeFleur. But she also understood Jim and Mrs. Ross's side of things. Taylor couldn't imagine how horrible it would be if for some reason she wasn't allowed to be around horses, especially Prince Albert and Pixie. Devon Ross knew Jim had a passion for horses, and she was just trying to help him.

If only the three of them could talk and tell one another exactly how he or she was feeling. Maybe they could come to some sort of understanding and fix this old feud.

"Wildwood is holding a winter carnival next weekend," Taylor said. "Maybe the two of you could come down. It's open to the public. You might catch Mrs. LeFleur in a good mood. Maybe you could straighten all this out."

"I doubt it," Jim disagreed. "It's been going on for too long. I think it's beyond repair."

"Mrs. LeFleur is a really great person," Taylor said sincerely. "And she's your mother. I think it would be a shame to miss out on having her back in your life, especially now that you live so close by."

"It's her choice," Jim said stubbornly. "Aunt Devon and I have tried."

"When did you say that carnival was?" Mrs. Ross asked Taylor.

"This Saturday. The money we raise will go toward helping the animals at the barn. We need supplies and food and things. It's a fund-raiser, and also a way of advertising Wildwood. Mrs. LeFleur is hoping it will make people more aware that the ranch is open again."

"I'm so glad she reopened the place," Mrs. Ross said. A faraway look came into her eyes. "It was such a wonderful place to grow up."

"It sure was," Jim agreed.

"Yeah," Taylor said. "And I can tell you, it's still the best place in the world."

Chapter 13

$\mathcal{G}$reat job, Katlyn!" Taylor praised the girl she was helping to get down from Pixie's saddle. Her mother had brought her in for a private lesson. "Adam has a cold," she'd explained.

The other girl from Taylor's first class, Sarah, had changed her lesson day to Wednesday. It meant that Taylor would be teaching Adam and Katlyn on Mondays and Sarah on Wednesdays. That would earn her enough money to pay her mother back and hopefully to buy her a nice Christmas gift.

"Let's see if you can dismount," Taylor told Katlyn.

The girl let herself fall from the stirrup into Taylor's arms. Taylor laughed as she tottered backward, holding Katlyn, who hung to her neck.

"Next week we'll do some more work on that dismount," Taylor said, smiling.

Taylor set Katlyn down gently. She gave her Pixie's reins, and together they walked to the corral gate.

Mercedes was working with two eleven-year-old boys, jogging alongside them as they rode Cody and Jojo at a walk around the perimeter of the corral.

"Heels down," Mercedes instructed. "Shoulders back. Keep your eyes looking between your horse's ears. Wherever you look, that's where he'll go."

Her voice sounded less strident and harsh than it had during her previous lesson. Was it possible she'd actually learned that she'd been too hard on the kids?

Unfortunately, Roberta Segarra hadn't returned at all. Mrs. LeFleur had to be aware that Mercedes had cost the ranch a potential boarding contract. Taylor wondered if Mrs. LeFleur had spoken to Mercedes about it.

Just before they were about to enter the main building, Taylor heard hammering and turned toward the sound. Travis was working on a plywood booth for the carnival. He looked up and waved to her.

"Is he your boyfriend?" Katlyn asked as Taylor waved back to Travis.

"No, he's my *best* friend," Taylor replied.

Katlyn pointed in the direction of the path to the upper pasture. "Is *he* your boyfriend?"

Eric was headed up the path on foot. Taylor realized he was going to check on Spots. Even if Spots came to the salt lick, Taylor didn't know how Eric was ever going to be able to catch him. It made her a little sad to think of Eric devoting himself to a task that was probably impossible. But it made her a little happy, too, to know he cared so much about Spots.

Taylor turned her attention back to Katlyn. "Are you coming to the carnival this Saturday?"

"Yeah! I told Adam he has to get better by then."

"I hope so," Taylor said. "It's going to be so much fun!"

The warm air of the main building felt good as they stepped inside. "Want to help me groom Pixie?" she asked the younger girl.

"Sure!" Katlyn agreed. "Can we braid her hair?"

"I guess so, once we get her all cleaned up." Taylor took the currycomb from the grooming box and handed it to Katlyn. "Remember how I showed you last time?"

"Uh-huh," Katlyn agreed as she made circles in the air with the brush.

"Very good," Taylor commended her.

Taylor and Katlyn were braiding Pixie's mane when Eric joined them. "Any sign of Spots?" Taylor asked him.

Eric's face lit with a smile. "Poop!" he said.

Katlyn giggled as Taylor shot him a quizzical glance. "What did you say?"

"There was deer poop near the salt lick! And the salt had definitely been licked," Eric reported.

"Great!" Taylor said. It was all she intended to say, but she just couldn't hold back. "Eric, how do you plan to catch Spots? I mean, even if he comes to the salt lick while you're there, won't it be just as hard to grab him as it was for Mercedes to lasso him?"

Eric rubbed the back of his neck thoughtfully. "Honestly, I don't know," he admitted. "I had this idea that maybe he had bonded with me since I fed him when he a little fawn, and he might just follow me back here. Don't laugh."

"I'm not laughing. I guess it's possible," Taylor said. "But even if he did come back, we'd have to send him away again. We can't keep a deer here."

"Why not?" Eric challenged, with just a hint of annoyance. "We keep horses here."

"But they're domesticated animals. A deer is wild."

"Didn't you just say the other day that Spots wasn't completely wild, that he couldn't survive in the woods on his own?"

"I was thinking of the sanctuary. Or we could help him along like you have been, but do a little more, like putting out food and water for him. There are sometimes coyotes in the woods, but Spots is getting big fast," Taylor argued. "I think coyotes go for smaller prey, and there's not much else out there to hurt him. Even the hunting is pretty restricted around here. Maybe he *could* survive with a little help."

Taylor could tell from the unhappy expression on Eric's face that he didn't like what he was hearing. But she felt she had to say these things. Being a friend didn't mean telling your pals only what they wanted to hear.

"Well, we'll see, I guess," Eric said. "I still think he might come with me."

"Maybe," Taylor allowed. She supposed anything was possible.

Just then, Travis stopped his work and walked over to join them. "Cool braid," he said to Katlyn.

"Thanks," she replied.

"I've got two booths built, only about a million more to build by Saturday," Travis joked to Taylor.

"Only a million?" Taylor teased.

"Yeah, that's all," Travis replied with a grin.

"I'll help you," Eric offered.

Taylor's eyes darted between Eric and Travis. Privately,

Travis claimed to dislike Eric. Would he accept the offer of help?

"Sure," Travis agreed. "Let's go. We can knock one more together before dark." Travis paused a moment. "Hey, I saw you up by the salt lick. Any sign of Spots?"

Taylor smiled softly to herself as Travis and Eric walked off together, discussing the possibility of Spots returning. Maybe Travis was softening toward Eric.

"That boy is your boyfriend," Katlyn remarked.

"No, he's not," Taylor told her.

"You like him," Katlyn observed. "Both of you like each other."

Taylor sighed. "Yes, we do, but not like you mean. He's not my boyfriend."

Mercedes came in, leading Cody and Jojo. "Can we groom them, too?" Katlyn asked excitedly.

Mercedes paused and seemed as though she was about to say no, but then something in her expression softened. "Actually, would you mind brushing down Cody, Taylor?"

The civility and politeness in her tone took Taylor by surprise. It was the first time Mercedes hadn't sniped at her or iced her out in days.

"No. It's no problem," Taylor agreed.

Taylor returned Pixie to her stall and tied Cody into the cross rings. Before Katlyn could pick up the curry-comb brush, though, her mother walked toward them, accompanied by Mrs. LeFleur.

"Mom! I'm grooming!" Katlyn shouted gleefully.

"I see that," her mother said with a smile. "How was your lesson?"

"I walked with no hands!" Katlyn chirped. Taylor had coached Katlyn to put down the reins and spread her arms wide, in order to give her a sense of the right balance in the saddle.

"That sounds fun," Katlyn's mother said.

"It was fun! Taylor does fun things, not like that other mean teacher."

Taylor sucked in a sharp breath as Mercedes walked up from the back of the stable. Her expression revealed that she'd heard Katlyn loud and clear.

"She didn't mean —" Katlyn's mother began to apologize to Mercedes.

"That's all right," Mercedes said before Katlyn's mother could finish. "The mean teacher needs to change — and she's going to."

Chapter 14

When Taylor awoke on Saturday morning, a delicious smell wafted into her bedroom. Sitting upright, she inhaled deeply. In the next second she had thrown off her quilt and was hurrying down the stairs to see what her mother was cooking.

"I want some of that, whatever it is!" Taylor announced when she got to the kitchen.

"It will cost you a dollar," her mother replied. She sat at the kitchen table surrounded by paper plates of chocolate chip cookies, brownies, and pretzels dipped in chocolate. At the end of the table were at least twenty glass mason jars, each one filled with ingredients layered on top of each other like colored sand in a bottle.

"See those squares of gingham cloth?" Jennifer said, pointing. "They all need to be placed on top of the jars, and then the lids need to be put on over them. And when that's done, those ribbons over there can be tied around the jars."

"What are they?" Taylor asked, sitting at the table.

"They're the dry ingredients for these brownies and cookies, measured out exactly. All a person has to do is add butter, eggs, and milk or water."

"These will sell out right away," Taylor remarked confidently.

"Have some breakfast first, and then would you help me with them? I have so much to do, and the carnival starts at ten. I still have to wrap all these cookies."

"Sure, I'll help, but it will cost you," Taylor replied.

Her mother made a face and sighed. "How much?"

"Brownies!" Taylor said with a laugh. She scooped one off the pile and took a large bite.

"Taylor!" her mother shouted. "Stop! You haven't even had breakfast."

"So? Who needs breakfast when there are brownies and cookies on the table?"

"You need breakfast, and I need help with this. Get yourself some cereal. We also have to go help Claire. She went to a shelter last night and came home with twenty puppies and kittens to try to adopt out today. I said we'd help her get them all together."

They had a lot of work ahead, but Taylor was excited. Today was going to be a fun day.

By nine that morning, Wildwood Stables was up and running. Jennifer had all her wares set out along with two silver urns, one for coffee and one for hot cider.

Transporting all the puppies and kittens was a big job, but fun. They were all so adorable. Eric, Travis, and Taylor couldn't stop laughing as they tried to get the exuberant and frisky animals into their wire cages.

"It's snowing!" Taylor realized as a fat flake of shining whiteness hit her nose.

Everyone gathered in front of the main building, faces to the sky, to marvel at the beauty of the winter's first snowfall.

"Will this stop people from coming to the carnival?" Travis worried.

"I hope not," Mrs. LeFleur said. "As long as it stays light and fluffy like this we should be all right. We'd better keep working so we'll be ready."

Mrs. LeFleur turned to go back into her office as everyone else dispersed. On an impulse, Taylor reached out to touch her elbow. Mrs. LeFleur turned. "What is it, honey?"

"When you get the money from the carnival, do you think there will be enough funds in there to — to — do you think you could buy some new horse blankets, and we could use one for Pixie and one for Prince Albert?"

Taylor's throat was dry. Had she annoyed Mrs. LeFleur with this request? After all, the woman had a whole ranch to run. Maybe now hadn't been the right time to bring it up.

To Taylor's relief, Mrs. LeFleur smiled. Reaching into the wide pocket of her barn jacket, she pulled out a folded piece of paper and handed it to Taylor. "Read it," Mrs. LeFleur advised.

The paper was headed: To Buy with Funds from Carnival. Taylor read down the numbered list until she got to item number five. "Two horse blankets needed for Prince Albert and Pixie," she read out loud.

"See, Taylor? They won't be shivering this winter."

Impulsively, Taylor threw her arms around Mrs. LeFleur. "Thank you. I've been so worried about them."

"Well, you can stop worrying," Mrs. LeFleur assured her. "Can you go inside and help Mercedes turn the horses out to the side paddock? We want everyone to be able to see our happy horses. You can help give horseback rides later, can't you?"

"Sure thing!"

Taylor walked into the main building with Mrs. LeFleur and kept going down the wide center aisle. She found Mercedes in Monty's stall, combing his mane.

"Who do you want me to bring out first?" Taylor asked.

"It doesn't matter," Mercedes said. "But wait," she added as Taylor turned to begin taking out horses. "I have something for you."

"For me? What?"

Mercedes wriggled a piece of paper from the back pocket of her jeans. "I'm giving this to you. It's a holiday gift."

Puzzled, Taylor unfolded the paper. Her jaw dropped when she realized what it was. Immediately, she thrust it back toward Mercedes.

"No. I can't take this. It's yours!"

Mercedes was trying to give her the prize she's won at the competitions — lessons with Keith Hobbes!

Mercedes pushed the paper back to Taylor. "I don't even want it," she said. "I just entered the competition to see how I'd do. I want to spend all my time here at the ranch working with Monty."

"But Keith is world famous," Taylor insisted. "You can't pass this up."

"Sure, I can," Mercedes disagreed. "Besides, it's also my way of saying I'm sorry about the way I've been acting. I've been a jealous jerk."

"It's okay. I forgive you. You don't have to give me your prize."

"Would you take it already!" Mercedes exploded. "You're starting to get on my nerves!"

Taylor laughed. This was the Mercedes she knew.

"Okay. I'm crazy happy to have this, if you're really sure about it," Taylor said.

"I'm positive."

Taylor wrapped Mercedes in a hug, but Mercedes immediately wriggled out of it. "Come on. We have to get those horses out into the side paddock before the people come. Let's get going!"

By ten-thirty the snow was sticking to the ground, and nearly an inch had fallen. Taylor's mother and Claire had moved their booths into the aisle of the main building.

Wildwood was gorgeous in the snow. Travis had set up a sound system, and holiday music now filled the air. Horseshoe toss stations and other games were set up.

But no one had arrived.

"The snow is keeping everyone away, just like you said," Taylor said to Travis.

"Here comes someone," Travis said, pointing.

"It's Daphne," Taylor said, recognizing the car.

The car stopped and Daphne got out. "I'm here to help," she announced cheerfully. Then she gazed around. "Where is everybody? I thought this started at ten."

"I think the snow is keeping everybody home. How are the roads?" Taylor asked.

"Not bad," Daphne reported. Suddenly, her eyes went wide. Taylor and Travis turned toward the upper pasture to see what had caught Daphne's attention.

"Is that who I think it is?" Taylor asked in a soft, awe-struck voice.

"Spots," Eric was crooning, his voice a near whisper filled with tenderness.

They'd all hurried through the falling snow to the upper pasture, afraid to startle the small deer that had come to the salt lick. There was no doubt at all that it was Spots. He was just the right size, with the same slightly crooked right ear.

When they were still yards away, Spots sensed their approach. His head shot up, and his ears jutted forward. The group froze, afraid that he would bolt.

"Eric, you should go up there alone," Daphne suggested. She reached into her jacket pocket and took out two apples. "Here," she said, offering them to Eric. "I brought these for the horses, but we need them now. They might entice him to come to you."

Eric took the apples and moved slowly forward alone. Taylor squeezed Daphne's arm anxiously. What would happen now?

Holding out one of the apples, Eric continued his approach. Spots seemed frozen in place. His ears flicked nervously, but he held his ground.

Spots took one wary step forward. Then another. Soon he was close enough to sniff the apple. Eric placed the apple on the ground and backed away, keeping his eyes on Spots.

Spots bit into the apple, shattering it into fragments with one bite.

When he was finished eating, he raised his head again. Eric and Spots seemed locked into a real connection. It lasted just a moment before Spots swung around and leaped toward the forest.

Eric wiped his eyes with a lightning-fast motion before turning back toward the group and smiling. "He knew me," he said.

They walked back down toward the main building. When they were halfway there, Mercedes met them, hands on hips. "Where have you guys been?" she scolded. "People are coming in like crazy!"

The group broke into a run. Cars were coming in fast. "Crank up the volume on that music," Taylor told Travis. "This carnival is on!"

All through the day, the snow kept up, but people kept coming. Taylor had never been busier. She dashed back and forth between helping with horse and pony rides and assisting Claire with her animal adoptions.

At about three o'clock, Taylor became aware that some large moving object was approaching the ranch from Wildwood Lane. It wasn't a car or truck because there was no motor sound.

"What's that?" Taylor asked Daphne who was standing nearby.

Daphne grinned at Taylor. "I know what it is. Come have a look," she added, running toward the approaching vehicle.

Taylor ran with Daphne and immediately saw what was coming. "You knew about this?" she cried.

"Yep. But I kept it for a surprise."

Jacques, the nearly white Percheron, was clip-clopping toward them, pulling a very large sleigh. He wore a necklace of bells that tinkled as he pulled the sleigh. Jim sat in the driver's seat, holding the reins.

In minutes, people began to gather, thrilled at the majestic sight. They walked near the sleigh until it stopped in front of the main building.

With a toss of his massive head, Jacques neighed a loud greeting.

Mrs. LeFleur stepped out of the main building to see what was going on. Taylor tensed. How would Mrs. LeFleur take this?

"Jim LeFleur, what mischief are you up to this time?" Mrs. LeFleur asked.

"I thought your guests might like a ride in a one-horse open sleigh," Jim replied. Reaching forward, he extended his gloved hand to her. "Could you find it in your heart to —" His voice caught with emotion and he hesitated. "Would you be the first to take a ride with me, Mom?" he continued. "Please."

Mrs. LeFleur stood still as if she was frozen in place.

Then she reached up and took her son's hand, allowing him to assist her into the sleigh. With a flick of the reins he prompted Jacques to carry them forward, toward the upper pasture.

"They're going to make up," Taylor said to Daphne. "I just know they are."

"People fight, but then they find their way back to each other, if they're lucky," Daphne said, and Taylor knew she was thinking of their fight.

"I feel lucky," Taylor told her with a smile.

And as the snow continued to fall, lucky was exactly what she felt. She felt incredibly lucky to have her friends and her family around her; lucky to have such a good life. So what if she didn't always get everything she wanted or have as much as someone like Plum? Taylor was grateful for everything — to be happy and healthy, loved and alive right here at Wildwood Stables, *the best place in the world.*

WILDWOOD STABLES

Stealing the Prize

SUZANNE WEYN

SCHOLASTIC

Stealing the Prize

Taylor Henry's life at Wildwood Stables is busier than ever. She's working with a new therapy horse program at the stables, practicing English-style riding, and still hoping to convince her horse, Prince Albert, to accept new riders. But when bratty Plum Mason brags about entering a jumping competition, Taylor can't resist taking on another project.

Plum insists on entering the show as a beginner—again. Unlike Plum, Taylor really is a beginner. But does she have what it takes to win?

Read them all!

Learning to Fly

Taylor Henry is finally learning English-style riding, just in time for elite Ross River Ranch's jumping competition. The grand prize is free riding lessons, and Taylor has her eye on the prize!

But it won't be a smooth ride to victory. Plum Mason is also entering the show, competing in Taylor's division. And learning to jump is much harder than Taylor had expected! It's time to take the reins—and a big leap of faith.

Racing Against Time

Taylor Henry and her horse, Prince Albert, are really settling in at Wildwood Stables. Prince Albert has even become a valuable therapy horse for a young girl with autism.

There's just one problem: Spoiled Plum Mason is always at Wildwood, too. Worse, she's overtraining her new horse, Shafir. Can Taylor and the other Wildwood girls keep Shafir safe? Or will Plum's suspiciously bad luck with horses strike again?

Playing for Keeps

Taylor Henry thinks Wildwood Stables is perfect—even if it needs repair and a lot more money, it's become a home to her and her new horse, Prince Albert. And as soon as Taylor trains Prince Albert to give lessons, Wildwood will be in business!

But the gelding refuses to let anyone ride him except Taylor. Can she convince Prince Albert to earn his keep? Or will Taylor need the help of her worst enemy to save her beloved new home?

You belong at

WILDWOOD STABLES

Daring to Dream

Taylor Henry loves horses, but her single mom can't afford riding lessons, much less a horse. So when she discovers an abandoned gelding and pony, Taylor is happy just to be around them.

But the rescued animals have nowhere to go, and Taylor is running out of time to find them a good home. Could the empty old barn on Wildwood Lane be the answer? And could Taylor's wildest dream—of a horse to call her own—finally be coming true?